CW00507505

Midnight Hexes And Hormonal Exes

Menopause, Magick, & Mystery, Volume 6

JC BLAKE

Published by Redbegga Publishing, 2022.

MIDNIGHT HEXES AND HORMONAL EXES

First edition. April 29, 2022.

Written by JC BLAKE.

To my family.

Chapter One

"I forgot to tell you, dear, but Millicent is arriving this afternoon." Aunt Beatrice didn't turn from the stove as she spoke. She lifted the kettle, a large wad of quilted hessian wrapped around the handle and poured boiling water into the waiting teapot.

Daring me to ignore him, Lucifer sat beside my aunt though his eyes were focused on me. The feline's glossy black fur, dark as a moonless midnight, seemed to sparkle as it reflected the kitchen's warm light. A fire burned low in the hearth, ash already collecting beneath the iron grate, proof of my aunts' industrious early mornings. Freshly baked bread sat cooling on a wire rack. More dough sat within a cloth-covered bowl, rising before the fire.

"Who is Millicent?" I asked, pouring water into Lucifer's saucer. He sniffed at the liquid, pushed it away with his paw then yowled whilst eyeing me with disdain. "There is no way that I am giving you port at this time in the morning, Lou!" I said in my best scolding-him-softly voice.

"You've made a rod for your own back there, Livitha." Aunt Thomasin stood in the kitchen doorway, the wide streak of pure white running through her glossy raven hair particularly outstanding this morning. Even this early, and despite the furry pink slippers – a prized gift from Uncle Raif last Yule - she looked immaculate in a long pencil skirt and floral shirt and was doing a bad job of looking the seventy-year-old she was supposed to be. It crossed my mind that she may have tinkered with magick to make herself appear younger. A wide belt sat tight around her slender waist. "Giving him salmon and port at the drop of a hat."

If Lucifer could have pursed his lips he would have. "I would be obliged if you could mind your own business, Mistress Thomasin." He threw a sideways glance at my aunt then sat in regal disapproval.

"Hark at him!" She sat down at the breakfast table and reached for a slice of toast, her wide silver bangle catching the light. "Spare the rod, spoil the child, Livitha."

Bacon sizzled on the stove, fire burned in the hearth, and Lucifer continued to sulk. I ignored him although knew that I would pay for this 'insolence' at some point in the near future.

Taking a seat opposite Aunt Thomasin, I reached for a thickly cut slice of toast from the rack and lathered it with butter—the diet could wait, plus I'd read that saturated fats weren't the real cause of heart disease, inflammation was, so plenty of butter was no longer bitten down upon with a serving of guilt. A low carb diet helped but giving up my morning hit was proving difficult.

"Did I hear you mention Millicent, sister?" asked Aunt Thomasin.

"Why yes, I told you the other day that she was coming today," replied Aunt Beatrice. Her full skirt swished as she moved to the fire and poked at the glowing logs, holding her apron away from the flames.

"You did not!"

"I did," she retorted, and moved back to the stove.

"I am quite certain that I would have remembered if you had told me that a visit from Millicent was imminent, dear sister." Aunt Thomasin pursed her lips, concentrating on Aunt

Beatrice as she busied herself with the bacon. She flipped the rashers, turned off the stove and slid them onto a waiting plate. Aunt Thomasin continued to watch as she approached the table, an unspoken accusation floating in the air. "What do you have to tell us, Beatrice?" she asked as the plate of bacon was placed upon the table. "You've been a little bit 'off' recently."

"Off? Why, I have no idea what you are referring to," she replied whilst taking great interest in the toast, butter, and bacon on the table. "We have eggs this morning," she said chirpily and removed the lid from a prettily decorated vintage tureen to reveal a large heap of creamy scrambled eggs. Like most of the items in the kitchen it dated back to the last century.

"Hmm," Aunt Thomasin took a sip of tea, the intricately decorated and wide silver bangle she always wore glinting in the bright sun shining through the window.

"It's bright today, but I think chilly." Aunt Beatrice took a bite of toast thickly spread with butter and marmalade, her hair a cloud of the richest auburn with flashes of white at the temples.

"Eat up, dears, there's much to do this morning."

Aunt Thomasin's lips pursed, and she shook her head in dissatisfaction. "She's hiding something from us, Livitha. I can always tell."

Aunt Beatrice made no response to this accusation and instead took a slice of bacon from the plate and then a heaped spoonful of eggs. "The hens are still laying, which is a blessing," she said.

There was no mistaking it, Aunt Beatrice was avoiding the conversation. "So," I said, "this Millicent-"

"Yes! Exactly! Millicent," blurted Aunt Thomasin

"Now, now. There is no need to be so dramatic, Thomasin."

"But you said nothing about her coming here today!"

"I'm sure I told you."

"You did not!"

I sighed. We were heading for a scene.

As Aunt Thomasin muttered something about being 'deceitful' Aunt Loveday stepped into the kitchen, her vibrant green eyes dancing with curiosity. This morning she had chosen to wear her hair down. Silvery-white and amazingly thick, it fell in full and luxurious curls. Dressed in black, slim-cut trousers and a shirt belted at the waist, she wore a hip-length cashmere cardigan in a silvery-blue that complemented her hair perfectly. Her skin, still smooth over high cheekbones, glowed. With a greeting of, 'Good morning, sisters,' she sat down at the table, filled her teacup then chattered about her plans for the day until footsteps in the hallway announced the arrival of Aunt Euphemia and then Uncle Raif.

Aunt Euphemia wafted the air as she entered the room, the oversized sleeve of her immaculately white tunic sweeping the air. Her heels clacked as she crossed the floor. "Oof! There's a tingle in the air this morning," she said whilst looking from aunt to aunt then took her place at the breakfast table. Like my other aunts, each in their unique way, she looked immaculate, and I envied her silvery-white cropped hair. Mine, a faded strawberry blonde, was dull in comparison, despite the streak of white it now sported.

Uncle Raif sat in the grandfather chair at the head of the table and placed a hand over Aunt Loveday's. She leaned to him as he placed a kiss on her cheek. Their displays of mutual affection were always charming, and I hoped that one day Garrett and I could live just as happily together. Aunt Loveday caught my gaze as she reached for the teapot to fill Uncle Raif's cup. Once again, both seemed full of vitality, their strength and health restored after the murderous attack by Hegelina Fekkit that had nearly killed them both.

Your time will come. Patience has its rewards.

The ancient voices that whispered to me were becoming more frequent, passing on snippets of knowledge but being patient where Garrett was concerned was something I was struggling with. Our time was now. Surely!

Since coming into my powers, Garrett had reappeared in my life. We were childhood sweethearts but somehow life had gotten in the way, and we had lost contact. I had married Pascal. We had been happy for a time, but his philandering had eventually destroyed our marriage and I'd realised that we were never really meant to be together. Garrett and I were different. We were soulmates. I could feel that. There was a bond between us that hadn't broken since the first day we met and now that we had found each other again, I yearned to be with him and, to my utter joy, he seemed to want the same thing too. That my aunts disapproved of me dating him had been a massive stumbling block, but they had come round to the idea, even told me that I must follow my heart in this situation; a lifetime of loneliness was a literal eternity to a witch and only corrupted our beings, so, loving, finding a mate among us, was preferable to being alone. I sighed as I watched Loveday and Raif, their gentle love radiating as they sat together.

The conversation, as was usual with my aunts, had meandered. "So," I said, watching carefully for the responses, "who is Millicent?"

Uncle Raif sighed, shook his head, and reached for a rasher of bacon. Aunt Euphemia raised her brows. Aunt Loveday frowned. Aunt Thomasin nodded her head and stared directly at Aunt Beatrice. "Beatrice tells me that she is visiting—this afternoon."

Uncle Raif groaned. "I'm afraid the garden beckons today, I have mulching to attend to whilst the weather still holds, so I hope you'll pass on my regards to Lady Millicent."

"Lady? Is she a noble then?"

Aunt Euphemia laughed. "Only in her own estimation. She bought some land, there was a title attached, she decided to use it."

"Just not the done thing," exclaimed Uncle Raif. "More honoured in the breach than the observance." He took a large spoonful of scrambled eggs then cut into his bacon. "That's a Shakespearian quote. Hamlet if I'm not mistaken. I met him once."

"Hamlet?"

"No," Uncle Raif chuckled. "The author, William. Nice chap."

"I remember him well, dear."

Uncle Raif nodded in agreement and then several quiet minutes passed as we ate our breakfast.

"With reference to Millicent," said Aunt Loveday. "We all have our failings."

"Pah!" exclaimed Aunt Thomasin. "You're too soft, Loveday."

"I did not know that Millicent was arriving this afternoon, Beatrice," Aunt Loveday continued. "I wish you had informed me earlier."

"Hah! I told you so," said Aunt Thomasin. "She did not tell us."

Aunt Beatrice shook her head. "Well, I thought I had."

"I wish you had," continued Aunt Loveday. "But I'm sure we can all agree to greet her well."

"Greet her well! After what she did?"

"That's in the past now, Euphemia."

"Well, she certainly climbed up the greasy pole of preferment."

Aunt Loveday nodded. "Indeed."

"More like clawed her way up it, standing on the slain bodies of her victims!"

"Oh, Euphemia, you have such a vivid imagination ... But ... do you think she really killed people to get where she is?"

"Well-"

Aunt Loveday raised a hand. "Now, let's not have any of this talk. Nothing was ever proven. And if she is coming here this afternoon," she glanced across at Beatrice, "then we need to cleanse the house."

"But it's lovely and tidy and Mrs. Driscoll will be here shortly," I said looking around. The Welsh dresser was stocked with plates, bottles, and bowls—all gleaming without a hint of dust. The fireplace was soot and ash free. Even the fire glowed in an attractively warm and gentle way. The floors were swept without hint of dirt building up against the skirting. The flagstone tiles were washed and would be cleaner by the afternoon once Mrs. Driscoll had finished her work. We had spent weeks cleaning through the house after our summer visitor and then Hegelina Fekkit's efforts at destroying it. Even the rugs had been taken out and given a thorough beating over the washing line. "She's worked so hard to prepare the house for winter. And she's still not right after her ordeal." Hegelina Fekkit had used dark magick to hide within Mrs. Driscoll and despite our best efforts at erasing the incident from her memory, she had momentary relapses and became confused. I'd found her on more than one occasion holding an item aloft, dazed, and unsure of reality.

"Not that kind of cleanse, dear. I mean an energy cleanse. We need to cleanse the house of the energy that is swirling around this kitchen. Millicent will pick up on it immediately, just as Euphemia did as she walked through the door; she will know that we have been talking about her and that her presence is a disruption."

"Disruption is putting it mildly."

"We must welcome her without prejudice."

"Are you scared of her?" I said with sudden realisation.

Five pairs of eyes fell on me. Silence followed for several moments.

"Well, she is in a position of great power."

"Power corrupts!" blurted Aunt Thomasin.

"Indeed."

"And the corrupt do terrible things."

"Now, now, sisters. Let's leave this for another time. This morning we must concentrate on cleansing the house ... and ourselves ... of this prejudicial ..."

"Oh, gadzooks, Loveday!" Uncle Raif sat back in his chair. "Enough of skirting around the subject. The woman is a termagant with a tyrannical imperative and I for one simply cannot stand her. If you'll excuse me ladies." He rose from the table. "I shall be in the garden this morning and will be taking a ride into town after luncheon. She is coming after luncheon is she not?"

Aunt Beatrice nodded.

"Then I shall visit Cedric. Yes, it's been a while." With that he kissed Aunt Loveday on the cheek and left the room.

Despite the glut of clues that Millicent was a woman to be feared, even despised, I was still unclear as to who she was. "I still don't know who Millicent is."

"She's the director of Hemlock Academy aka The Academy for Advanced Witchcraft. She is Beatrice's new boss."

"Head crone of all the covens."

"I will never recognise her as such. That election was fraudulent. There is something rotten there."

"Nevertheless, she was recognised and inaugurated, so we must treat her with the respect that office deserves."

"So if she is this high and mighty person, why is she coming here?"

"Beatrice?"

Aunt Beatrice shrugged. "I'm not sure. I was just informed that she was coming. I think it has something to do with Livitha."

"Me!"

"Thor's hammer, Beatrice!" exclaimed Aunt Loveday. "Whatever is going on?"

Chapter Two

The air in the kitchen crackled with fractious energy as the front door swung open, closed, and was followed by the unmistakable clack of Mrs. Driscoll's shoes and rustle of her water-resistant overcoat. Aunt Beatrice left the table to busy herself at the sink and Aunt Thomasin began to collect the plates.

"Good morning, ladies!" Mrs. Driscoll stepped into the kitchen oblivious to the tension within the room. "Such a beautiful day today. I see Raif is already busy outside. Can't say I blame him; I'm itching to get to my flower beds and tidy up those wilting stems. It's been such terrible weather of late that I just haven't been outside and there are leaves everywhere. My Patrick would have scolded me rotten. Oh, yes, he would." She continued to chatter about her late husband whilst collecting her trug of cleaning products and cloths from the cupboard beneath the sink and then disappeared into the hall. She often spoke of him and each time I was reminded of his death and how he had suffered a massive coronary whilst manoeuvring a forklift laden with pallets, crashing into a display of garden gnomes. The poor man had been dead before the last broken gnome, head severed from its body, had come to a rolling stop beside the forklift.

"Well, Beatrice. You have some explaining to do," Aunt Thomasin demanded as soon as Mrs. Driscoll was out of earshot.

"I don't know anything other than she'd like to talk to Livitha."

"Why on earth would she want to talk to Livitha?"

"It's obvious," said Aunt Loveday. "She's headhunting."

"She can't have Livitha's head!"

"Don't be silly, Euphemia. I mean that she is likely recruiting for her dratted Academy."

Aunt Beatrice huffed. "The Academy does important work, Loveday. Only this summer I helped Maximus Blackwood find a new Keeper."

"Ooh!" said Euphemia. "You didn't tell me about that?"

"Well ... I'm not meant to tell. It's part of the contract."

"Summer, Beatrice? I wasn't aware that you were working for the Academy during the summer. You made no mention of it. Surely, we should have been told?" challenged Aunt Loveday.

"Well, I was told not to tell."

"And have you been spying on us then?"

Aunt Beatrice turned to Aunt Thomasin; her widened eyes carried a flicker of indignation flecked with pain. "No! Of course not. It's just ... the work is, so I was told, of a sensitive nature."

"Well, as head of this coven," Aunt Loveday said with seriousness. "I suggest, no insist, that we convene a meeting and discuss this. Beatrice working for the Academy affects us all."

"I'm not sure I like it," said Aunt Thomasin.

"Nor I," added Aunt Euphemia.

Aunt Beatrice pursed her lips. "Very well. Convene a meeting."

"Thank you, Beatrice. I feel it is something that cannot be kept a secret from us. Haligern coven takes priority over Hemlock Academy."

"Yes, of course."

The conversation halted and my aunts busied themselves in the kitchen as the noise of the vacuum cleaner ceased and Mrs. Driscoll reappeared.

"I'm parched, ladies. I know it's early, but shall we have a cup of tea?"

This was a signal that Mrs. Driscoll had some gossip she wanted to share and despite having only just finished breakfast my aunts readily agreed to another cup of tea. Aunt Beatrice swilled out the tea leaves from the pot and made a fresh brew whilst Mrs. Driscoll took out the broom and swept the floor. Minutes later, the pot of tea sat steaming at the centre of the table beside a plate of freshly made biscuits.

"Shall I be Mother?"

"Go ahead, Thomasin."

Aunt Thomasin poured the tea and the conversation once again turned to the weather as we waited for Mrs. Driscoll to begin. We didn't have to wait long.

"Such a lovely day," she said whilst glancing out of the window. She took a biscuit from the plate. "You wouldn't know that such horrors were happening right on our doorstep."

This was going to be juicy! "Horrors?" I asked.

"On our doorstep?"

"Oh! Haven't you heard?"

We agreed that we had not. I watched Mrs. Driscoll closely; she was revelling in being the first to tell us.

"Well, it's such a terrible thing! Out on the moor ..."

"Yes?"

"They found the body of a woman and she had been *mauled* to death. Mauled!" she repeated.

"On the moor, you say," said Aunt Loveday. "Which moor would that be?"

There were a number of moors in the local area.

"Wolfstane Moor!" she said, her eyes shining. "They do say it was an animal that did it. The poor woman was shredded. That's what I've heard. Penny Arbuckle's husband works for the police, and she said that he'd said the woman was barely recognisable." Mrs. Driscoll gave a theatrical shudder. "Just doesn't bear thinking about. Shredded is the word she used. Shredded!" She took another sip of tea then a bite of her biscuit, allowing her revelations to sink in.

"Hideous!" exclaimed Aunt Thomasin.

"Poor woman," said Aunt Beatrice.

"A terrible way to go," agreed Aunt Loveday.

My aunts made the appropriate noises of being shocked and horrified but there was something disingenuous about their response.

"Who was she?" I asked, fending off the image of a woman's 'shredded' corpse strewn across the heather.

"A walker, they think. Her car was parked at the side of the road and her body was found mutilated! Mutilated! Can you imagine what the poor woman went through? Ripped to shreds! Just terrible! And so close to home."

Wolfstane Moor was less than five miles away.

Concerned glances flitted between my aunts. "Yes, that is dreadful," Aunt Loveday said whilst absentmindedly twisting her bangle.

"It is," agreed Mrs. Driscoll. "And of course, they're saying that the Beast of Wolfstane Moor has returned."

This drew a gasp from Aunt Euphemia.

"Surely not, that was such a long time ago."

"It is, but people have long memories."

"I thought that he had been caught."

"They did and it was PC Ernest Idle who caught him. It was him that put all the pieces together. Such a shock for the village. You must know his daughter Karyn. She married well—Neil Montpellier. Now there's money in *that* family and he's an accountant, and they always have plenty of money. Didn't you go to school with her, Livitha?"

"Karyn Idle? Oh, yes, I did." I remembered Karyn. "She was at school with me when the murders happened, and I remembered her bragging about how her dad was on the case. "She's on the Parish Council now, isn't she?"

"Oh, yes. She's done so well for herself. She owns a business and is on the Parish Council too."

We sat in silence for several moments. I had vague memories of newspaper articles and photographs of the girl murdered on the moor. She had been of a similar age to me at the time and a wave of shock had rippled through our community.

"Well, if he is in prison, it is most likely to be an animal," said Aunt Loveday. Her statement was quickly seconded by Aunt Thomasin and followed by murmurs of agreement from my other aunts.

"Could it be *the* Beast of Wolfstane Moor?" asked Mrs. Driscoll. "It doesn't seem possible, but there are so many strange things in the world, and there is the legend, obviously."

"Oh, that's just a legend," said Aunt Loveday quickly.

"I'm sure it's just an animal—perhaps a dog," added Aunt Thomasin.

"What kind of dog shreds a person?" I asked.

"It's bound to be an exaggeration, dear. You know how people love to embellish a story."

"It's what I was told," said Mrs. Driscoll. "And it's what the police are saying." Mrs. Driscoll sipped her tea without further comment.

"Is that what people are saying? That it's a werewolf up on the moors?" asked Aunt Thomasin.

"Some have talked about it. Mr. Brocklethwaite was talking about making some silver bullets although he's always had some odd ideas. He thought the village had been infested with vampires over the summer." She laughed. "Imagine that! Silly old man."

My aunts exchanged glances and Aunt Loveday spluttered then began to cough.

"Are you alright, Loveday," Mrs. Driscoll asked with concern.

"Yes." She coughed once more. "Sorry, ladies. My tea went down the wrong way."

"Well, I for one don't believe in this story of the Beast of Wolfstane Moor, it's a myth and probably one started to keep people off the land—something like that," explained Aunt Euphemia.

Again there were murmurs of agreement.

"I daresay you're right, ladies." Mrs. Driscoll sighed. "But I, for one, won't be going up on those moors any time soon and shall be keeping a close watch on Agnes. She has a terribly overactive imagination, and it would be just like her to go up their beast-spotting."

"Oh, no, she really mustn't do that!" said Aunt Thomasin with a glance at my aunts. They nodded their heads in agreement.

"You know what they're like. She has a YouTube channel now. No doubt she would love to livestream the content. That's how they speak!" Mrs. Driscoll shook her head then took a final sip of tea and stood up. "So different than from when we were young. Well, the house won't clean itself," she said and stood up to leave.

"I'll join you. Shall we tackle the drawing room first?"

"Yes, Beatrice and then I'm planning on blitzing the bathrooms."

The two women continued to chatter about their plans to clean the house and Aunt Euphemia promised to join them. With three aunts remaining in the kitchen the mood became sombre.

"Do you really think that the Beast has returned, Loveday?" Aunt Euphemia asked.

For several moments, Aunt Loveday sat deep in thought, twisting the bangle at her wrist. "It's not impossible although I imagine that the incident has been greatly exaggerated. Mrs. D does love a good drama."

"But the beast is just a myth, isn't it?" I asked.

Aunt Loveday shook her head. "I'm afraid not dear. The Beast is, or at least was, very real, although he hasn't reared his head for ... well, more than fifty years. Oh, before you were born."

"So," I said, "the beast Mrs. Driscoll spoke of can't have been the one who killed that girl when I was a teenager."

"That's correct. The locals did refer to the killer as the 'Beast', but it was not the Beast *we* know that killed the girl—that was a case of ... well, horrible, but all too common I'm afraid."

Aunt Loveday glanced out of the window. "The morning is moving along, isn't it time that you were in the shop?"

I glanced at my watch. Nine-thirty am. The shop opened at ten. "Oh, heck! Yes." With unanswered questions, and a head full of dangerous creatures - Millicent among them - I left Haligern Cottage for our apothecary shop in the village.

Chapter Three

Despite the brightness of the morning, a thick fog hung low in the air covering the surrounding farmland, making my journey to the village frustratingly slow. As the car left Haligern woodlands and climbed through the undulating countryside that surrounded our land the fog sat as a massive bank, the sun bright above it. At the top of the hills it cleared but quickly thickened as I motored into another trough. Several miles outside of the village the fog had cleared enough to see across the fields where, shrouded in mist, a grouping of vans, cars, and 4x4s emerged. Beyond the cars were a number of caravans arranged in a large circle. "The gypsies are back," I murmured as I passed, the scene disappearing as the mist thickened once more. I hadn't gone much further when a figure, only just discernible, emerged from the fog.

Wearing a hi-vis neon pink vest was a woman with blonde hair pulled back into a tight ponytail that swung as she jogged along at a good pace. She appeared to be about my age but there the comparison ended. Where I was short and well-padded, she was tall, lithe, and sinewy, her skin tanned, her legs muscular. She seemed barely out of breathe, taking each stride easily even though we were miles from the village ahead and even further from the town behind. She could, of course, live in one of the isolated farmhouses that dotted the area. Envious, I watched as she ran past the car then disappeared back into the fog. Telling myself that I was built for comfort and not for speed and, promising to make more effort at avoiding starchy carbs, I made my way to the village and the shop.

In the village the mist had cleared, and I managed to park the car and unlock the door just as the ancient grandfather clock struck ten. The wheeze of its chimes was accompanied by the distinct chitter of fairies and, as the door closed behind me, noticing too late the approach of a customer, several tiny creatures flitted around the room, their irritation obvious. They were becoming far bolder and less skittish around me and although I wasn't completely calm in their presence, I had become used to them. One in particular, a male with a shock of white hair that danced around his head like the seedhead of a dandelion, had decided that it was his job to help me in the shop and although having him around was often more of a hindrance than a help, he had his uses. However, with the customer at the door and the fairies still flitting, swooping, and chittering as I placed my bag on the counter, I quickly shooed them.

"Hide! There's someone coming." I gestured for them to disperse. Behind me the doorbell tinkled and the last fairy, my friend with the shock of white hair, disappeared into the grandfather clock. Buzzing emanated from inside its chamber and once again it chimed. I took a breath and turned to face the customer with my best so-glad-you're-here-and-how-can-I-help-you smile.

"Good morning," I said chirpily.

"Is it?" The woman frowned and held my gaze.

I restrained a groan. This wasn't the first time the lady had been into the shop. I retained my smile and glanced through the window. "Oh, yes, it's a beautiful day."

She huffed. "Foggy and damp," she countered.

"The sun will burn it off and then it will be a beautiful day."

"I doubt that. It's cold."

I didn't want to disagree with the woman; previous efforts at challenging her relentless pessimism had resulted in a whining monologue that had cleared the shop. "You're right," I agreed. "But let's hope the sun warms us soon."

She huffed again and gestured to the log burner at the back of shop. "You should have put that on."

"It's on my list of jobs to do."

"You should have come in earlier and put it on then I wouldn't be standing here cold. What kind of shop makes its customers cold?"

I took a breath. "You're right," I said. "I'm late in this morning."

The woman moved to the large dresser filled with jars and bottles of lotions and potions. After several minutes of picking up a variety of bottles and reading the labels, she grumbled with dissatisfaction then moved to another shelf. I stacked the log burner with kindling and some screws of newspaper and lit the fire. The kindling and paper caught quickly, and I placed a log into the burner; the room would soon warm.

As I returned to the main shop, the woman caught my eye. It was obvious that she wanted to speak but she turned back to the shelf and picked up another bottle. Instead of ignoring her, I walked to her side. "Is there anything I can help you with?" I asked gently.

She huffed, replaced the bottle on the shelf, then turned to me. This time there was no hint of challenge in her eyes. "Well, actually, there is." She glanced to the shop door and then, in a lowered voice, said. "I'm … I've been off … of late." Her cheeks, already a little ruddy, grew red. "I do have a problem."

"Give me a moment." I locked the door, turned the sign to 'closed' then returned to her.

To my surprise she smiled. "Thank you. It's so embarrassing and I don't know who to get help from."

"I'll help if I can," I said.

"I ... I think I'm going through," she leaned into me then said in a low, conspiratorial tone, "the change." Looking at me with wide, appealing eyes.

"Me too." I offered her a smile. "It's awful, isn't it. I have to check my moustache every morning. I'm thinking about getting wax to make the ends twist upwards." I pinched the ends of an imaginary moustache.

"You too?" She looked at me in astonishment whilst scanning my upper lip for the non-existent moustache. Her lips curved to a smile, and she pushed out a loud breath then a relieved laugh. "But you look so ... lovely and healthy and young and there's not a hair on your chin!" She stroked at her own and I noticed a few thicker hairs at the side of her top lip as well as beneath her chin.

"That's only because I check for them, and ..." I couldn't tell her about the magick in the potions I took, "and I use some of our products. They ease the symptoms."

"Symptoms?" she urged.

"Well, I don't know about you, but I get terrible sweats at night, hot flushes during the day, sometimes I get cranky to the point of spontaneous combustion."

"Hah! Me too." Relief emanated from the woman, her dreary energy dissipating.

I would have to cleanse the shop once she'd left but if I managed this situation well then knew I could help her. Not for the first time I got a sense of the good that I could do with my new knowledge.

"We sell quite a lot of this to women like us," I said picking up a jar. It helps with hot flushes." I spent the next minutes going through the products we produced that were specifically for the menopause, pleased that I'd spent the time researching the problems women face and discovering what collective knowledge my aunts and their centuries old grimoires held that could soothe menopausal symptoms. Half an hour later the woman left the shop with a smile on her face and a bag filled with Haligern Apothecary concoctions, transformed from the grudging pessimist that had walked in. I sighed in satisfaction.

With the bright winter sun now streaming in through the windows and the log burner heating the room, I busied myself dusting and restocking the shelves then burned a stick of cleansing mugwort and lavender whilst I waited for other customers. Although the morning was slow, with only one other customer popping in to purchase a jar of anti-ageing moisturiser, the shop became busy during the afternoon, and I managed to sell a substantial amount of stock. Our anti-ageing creams were still doing extremely well and, alongside the women who came into the shop, email orders were picking up too.

A lull in business was broken by another customer, this time, a man. It was unusual for a man to come into the shop, so I was intrigued when he came straight to the counter and then began to talk in a furtive fashion after checking that the shop was empty and that no one was about to enter.

"I need something for my wife," he said with another glance at the door. "She's not ... well, she seems under the weather."

"We have a number of wonderful tonics that may be suitable, but it would help if you could give me some more information. Does she have symptoms?"

"Well, she keeps biting my head off!" he said in a rush. "And she's ... well, she's not interested in ... me." His cheeks held the beginning of a flush. "If you know what I mean."

"Erm."

"What I mean is ... she won't ... you know, have a cuddle, and it's not like her. We used to have a good marriage, but these last months ... She's very stressed. We've got a lot going on what with her father and the business and then there's that blasted Parish Council! She goes running so is as fit as a fiddle, and it always used to de-stress her, but even that's not helping with it these days." His face was now fully flushed. "I don't like to share personal details, but you come highly recommended." He raised his brows in a co-conspiratorial fashion. "Do you have anything for *stress* for women?"

I had to hold back a smile. "Stress of a particular variety?"

He nodded. "Yes! Stress women get at a certain age. She's making my life hell and if I mention going to the doctor or make any mention that perhaps she's going through the 'change' well, she can whip me with her tongue at a hundred paces!"

She sounded monstrous. "Can I ask how old she is?"

"She has her fiftieth birthday next month."

"It does sound like it could be the menopause," I said. "And we do have a variety of lotions and elixirs that could help."

He nodded with enthusiasm. "Load me up. I want it all!"

I felt a wave of sympathy for the man. It was a struggle for me to cope with my erratic hormones, but it sounded like this woman was having a worse time and her struggle was landing on her husband.

We spent the next minutes discussing her symptoms and I asked more questions about his wife and tried to tailor the items to her needs. "Obviously, it would be easier if she were to come in herself-"

"Oh, she'll never do that!"

"Do you think she'll accept this from you?"

He looked thoughtful. "Perhaps not ... but if you sent it!"

"Me?"

"Well, it's her birthday next month. You could send it from the shop ... and say that it's a birthday gift as a thank you for all the hard work she has done for the village. I know that she gave you permission to renovate this place."

"She's on the Planning Committee?"

He nodded. "Oh, yes. She's got her finger in all the pies. She works hard, but sometimes it's too much. Take this murder. You'd think it was her job to catch whoever did it—she's that worked up about it. She thinks it's the killer who murdered that teenager all them years ago. You're about the same age. Do you remember it?"

I nodded. "I do."

"Then you probably know my wife—Karyn Montpellier. Her dad worked on the case. He helped put the killer away."

"Ah! Yes, Karyn. She was in my class at school."

His smile broadened. "Well, you'll remember it all then."

"It made an impact at the time. The poor girl who died was a similar age to us."

"Dreadful business and Karyn has always been so proud that her dad was the one to help catch the killer and get him convicted."

"I do remember. We had insider knowledge. Karyn used to tell us what was going on, so we knew before it was in the papers."

"Well, she's up in arms about it again. You see, the problem is that they've let the killer out—on a technicality! She's beside herself. It besmirches her dad's memory you see, he passed last year."

"I'm sorry to hear that."

"It was a blow. He was a good man. Couldn't have asked for a better father-in-law and Karyn doted on him. She's taken the killer being let out badly. They're investigating her dad you see. Rumour has it that someone tampered with the evidence in the original case."

"I didn't realise he'd been let out. We thought the walker had been killed by an animal."

He shook his head. "Poor Heather! Dreadful business."

"You knew her?"

"We both did. She was a teacher at the local school, retired, but a friend of the family although we'd drifted apart of late. So, what with her hormones and then all of this," he made a circle with his arms as though encompassing our conversation, "she's struggling."

"I can see why. I'll add a little calmative to the 'gift'," I smiled.

"Marvellous!"

"Shall I send it early?" I asked.

"That would be kind of you."

"We're happy to help; it's what we're here for," I smiled. I jotted down the elixir on the list of items to be included in the birthday hamper then entered them into the till. The husband paid, wrote down the address, and I promised to deliver them to his wife myself.

It only took a few minutes after the man had gone for the wave of satisfaction I'd felt at being able to help fade as the gravity of his words sank in. It *was* possible that a serial killer was on the loose, one who targeted women, and one who was far too close to home for the danger to be ignored.

The afternoon sped by but despite a flow of easy-going and happy customers I was anxious to leave and couldn't shift the sense of foreboding that had sat with me since the conversation with my aunts this morning. A woman being murdered on the moors, savaged by some animal or insane psychopath, was bad enough, but what really bothered me was the impending visit from Millicent. That she was someone to be feared was obvious from my aunts' reaction to the news of her visit and that she was visiting because of *me* filled me with dread. Why? What on earth could she want with me? What had I done wrong? Was this another test?

With the shop empty, I turned my attention to the newest orders received by email and began to collect the items. News must be spreading about our new line of products for 'the change' as there were several emails asking for specific products that would help with menopausal symptoms – a sure sign that word of mouth was helping business. The fairy with the shock of white hair hovered at my shoulder, chittering, then swooping. There weren't many jobs that the tiny creature could do, and I was scrabbling for ideas to keep him busy (and not interfering) when the bell tinkled again, and another customer walked through the door. The fairy instantly retreated behind me, chittering in a distressed fashion, then dropped beneath the counter.

I placed a jar of rejuvenating night cream complete with drops of Aunt Thomasin's serum, a concoction of flowers and herbs collected under a gibbous moon whilst reciting an ancient charm, in a waiting box and pushed it to one side. I hated being ignored when shopping, so made my best efforts to be welcoming and attentive to everyone who walked through our door.

"Afternoon," I said whilst offering a smile.

The woman nodded then held my gaze, staring at me with an intensity that was immediately unsettling. The woman's aura grew visible; iridescent bands of violet and fuchsia grew to a dark purple around the outline of her body. I had never seen an aura as colourful before. The energy she threw off was intense and carried with it a sense of danger.

"Can I help you?" I asked glancing beyond her to the street outside; it was empty.

"No, but I can help you," she said.

Beneath the counter the fairy whimpered.

Chapter Four

The woman stood before me, aura shimmering. With dark hair hanging free to her waist, braids held by silver beads either side of her face, she wore a long and flowing top in dark red velvet embroidered with vibrant colours at the collar and cuffs, held in at the waist with a wide leather belt, tooled with intricate designs. She held out a hand, palm flat.

"If there's something in particular, you'd like ... perhaps some moisturiser? We do a soothing range of bath oils." I was rambling whilst my mind took in the vision before me. The woman seemed to wax and wane with subtle changes in her clothing, one version overlapping another. I blinked to clear my eyes, unsure of what I was seeing.

"There is nothing I want." Her voice was accented, reminding me of Vlad and his now ex-wife Martha, who still ran the shop just a few doors down from the apothecary. The thought that perhaps Martha could come to my rescue flitted across my mind, but it was still daylight so unlikely, verging on impossible, that she would be available.

"There is only one that can help you. The nightwalker is not she."

She had read my mind! "The nightwalker?" I ventured. Was this woman a witch? She had to be.

"The beautiful one. She is here, in this village. I sense her. I sense you reaching out to her."

I decided to play ignorant. "I'm not sure what you mean."

"The vampire. She is here. She is not the one you need."

"Oh. Well …" Schooled by my aunts to keep the details of our life, of who we really were, on a need-to-know basis, I fumbled with my words then shrugged my shoulders. The woman was a stranger, a particularly unusual one with magical powers, and I had no idea whether she was friend or foe.

She continued to hold out her hand, palm upwards. At its centre was a tattoo, its lines smudged where the ink had bled over time, but the design was clear – a protective rune, similar to the ones carved into the trees at Haligern cottage.

"That must have hurt," I said and gestured to the tattoo. "What does it mean?"

She made no effort at replying, instead she said, "Cross my palm with silver and I shall tell your fortune."

A gypsy?

"That's right."

"I'm not sure I want my fortune telling, thanks. Aunt Thomasin reads tea leaves and-"

"Pah!" She spat on the floor.

"Hey! That's not okay!" I chided.

She thrust her hand at me. "You are alone here. There is no one coming to your aid." She held my gaze. Her eyes, rimmed by kohl were a dark chestnut flecked with amber. "I know what you are, lady. Cross my palm with silver and I will tell you what you need to know."

"I-"

Listen to the gypsy witch. Listen to her wisdom. Harbinger of doom.

"Yes, listen."

A chill ran down my spine. Like my aunt, the woman had the gift of listening to others' thoughts so it was also likely that she had hidden powers and, given the sense of danger that I was picking up from her, I decided to listen to the advice of the ancient voices.

"So ... you're a witch?" I ventured.

She smiled to reveal a row of small and perfectly white teeth. "I am."

"And you're a gypsy?"

Again she smiled. "Good, now we are getting somewhere. Come! Cover my palm with silver."

I opened the drawer and took out a bag of fifty pence coins. I placed them in her hand. She spat on the floor.

"Hey! Just stop that. If you don't like something, just say. I've got to clean that mess up!"

"Feisty!" she said. "I like this. It is good. You will need this spirit." She handed me the bag of coins. "I said silver. It is silver that we need."

The only item of silver in the shop was the narrow bangle on my wrist bought on a trip to Paris with Pascal. It was a reminder of happier times.

She pointed to my wrist. "Yes, that will do."

"But it's mine."

"It is."

"It has ... sentimental value."

She grabbed my hand, squashing my fingers whilst staring into my eyes, her lips thinned. "Those memories are toxic to you. Let them go! The future is what matters." She threw my hand down. "Now," she said and once again held out her tattooed palm, "cross my palm with silver."

As I laid the silver on the gypsy-witch's palm, she sucked in her breath and closed her eyes, her fingers closing around the bracelet. The white-haired fairy rose to my side, hovering close to my shoulder it's chitter now a whisper. Heartbeat racing, one hand clutched by the gypsy witch, I watched as she swayed, confused and a little dazed at her demanding presence. The fairy landed on my shoulder then pushed through my hair to stand beside my neck using my ear as an anchor. Only last month I would have squealed with fright but now his presence was a comfort even if he was using me as a hiding place.

The swaying stopped and the woman stood still though her eyes remained closed. Breath caught in my chest. With the fairy at my ear, its tiny fingers like pinpricks in my lobe, I waited. She opened her eyes, and I caught the flicker of fear. A bead of sweat appeared at her brow.

She released my hand.

"What is it?"

She held up a hand to ward off my questions. Once again, I grew quiet and waited.

The tick from the grandfather clock grew loud.

"It is as I dreamt." She narrowed her eyes, capturing mine with hers. "Livitha, daughter of Soren, there is betrayal in your life." She watched for my reaction.

"I-"

Again she held up a silencing hand. "Let me speak of your future path—your fate. What will be will be. Nothing can stop it. There is betrayal that will lead to death. Betrayal that will lead to life. Betrayal that will uncover centuries of dark doings." She leant forward. "Blood! There is blood on the moors. Pain and suffering and loss and yearning." She gasped and took a step back. "The dark one comes." The bead of sweat at her hairline tracked down her forehead and she staggered, all colour draining from her face. I realised that she was about to faint and moved beside her, sliding my arm across her slender back. She crumpled against me. The fairy chittered in annoyance, its arms and legs tangled in my hair, then pushed its way out into the open. It flitted around me. Several others joined it and winged their way down to the counter as I sat the woman in a chair. She smelled of charcoal fires and vanilla, a peculiar but distinct combination. "The beast is waiting for you, Livitha. He waits and he knows what has passed. He wants you-" Her words tailed off and she sank into unconsciousness.

I propped her in the chair, a stone sinking in my stomach. People claimed that a woman had been slaughtered on the moors by the Beast of Wolfstane Moor and now this harbinger of doom claimed that the Beast was my fate! I shuddered as the fairies grew bold and began to flit around the gypsy-witch.

The clock struck the hour, its wheezing chimes ringing five times, and I remembered that I was expected back at the cottage for an audience with Millicent. The day had started badly, had nosedived, and was about to become worse. The sense of foreboding that had dogged me all day notched up to full blown anxiety. What did it all mean? A betrayal that would lead to death *and* life? A betrayal that would uncover deception and a deadly beast that was on the prowl and looking for me?

The woman began to stir then sat up with a start.

"Are you alright?" I asked with genuine concern. The woman's aura, so bright and energised when she had walked into the shop, was now faded and barely visible. Her face remained pale; sallowness tinged her complexion.

"A drink of water would be a kindness," she said.

The fairies flittered above her head then followed me to the small kitchen at the back of the shop. I filled a glass with water but as I turned off the tap the doorbell tinkled and when I returned the woman had gone. The sense of foreboding remained, and I locked up for the night, certain that the meeting with Millicent would only bring further dread news.

Chapter Five

At home, soft chatter and laughter emanated from the drawing room but the energy within the house was far from calm. As I'd travelled home along the winding roads, Millicent had grown in threat within my mind, the thick fog adding to my sense of vulnerability. Noticing the diffused lights of the gypsy caravans shining through the fog as I'd passed had not helped. Strained laughter within the drawing room grew loud as I opened the door.

"Ah, Livitha, there you are. We have been waiting on you."

In my mind Millicent had become a monstrous figure; the wicked witch from the *Wizard of Oz* with a side serving of the Child Catcher from *Chitty Chitty Bang Bang*. But before me, seated in Aunt Loveday's favourite highbacked armchair, warmed by the glowing fire, sat a petite woman with a pretty face and a friendly smile. A little on the plump side she would not have looked out of place with a pair of knitting needles in her hands and a kitten playing with the ball of wool at her feet. For a fleeting second, I imagined that a replacement had been sent to assess me. Certainly, this woman did not look like a crone to be feared.

In the quiet spaces during the day, before my mind had been completely distracted by the gypsy-witch and her prophecy, I had thought hard about what the Academy could want with me. I had come up with nothing that assuaged my concern. In fact, I could only think of negative reasons as to why they'd want to interrogate me. My witchy powers were nowhere near as under control as I, or my aunts, had hoped they would be by now, so it was unlikely I was being 'headhunted' as Loveday had suggested. Instead, I had become convinced that they were deciding if I were to be put on their delinquent witch programme or perhaps something worse!

I hid my surprise and smiled to the room. "Good evening."

The woman stood and offered me a friendly smile. "Livitha," she said without waiting for an introduction. "It is so good to finally meet you. I have heard much of your travails."

I held back the internal sigh. Did they all know about my disastrous marriage and accusations of murder? Of course they did.

Despite the outward friendliness, Aunt Loveday bristled, and my aunts hid their disapproval behind fixed smiles. As soon as the woman spoke, coven etiquette had been breached; it was for Aunt Loveday to make the introductions. However, the woman was warm and friendly without hint of attempting to assert her dominance. "Come forward child," she said whilst squinting, "and let me have a good look at you."

I stepped forward and took her outheld hand. That was my first mistake. Our hands locked and I was overwhelmed by the sensation of being 'read' as I felt the woman's mind within my own, like prodding fingers pressing down into a pillow. I reeled as topaz irises glittered and smiling eyes locked to mine but forced my mind to block her efforts. Her eyes narrowed and then she dropped my hand. I gasped.

"Shocking!" muttered Aunt Thomasin.

Aunt Beatrice gave her a warning nudge with her elbow, lips pursed.

The fixed smiles remained and for the first time I sensed fearful energy among my aunts.

"Livitha, may I introduce Millicent, Director of the Academy of Advanced Witchcraft."

"And don't forget that I am also the General Secretary of the Witches' Institute." She threw Loveday a friendly smile. She looked like a sweet old lady, someone who would always have a slice of Victoria sponge ready and waiting for visitors, of whom there would be many, given her pleasing disposition.

It was an intensely disingenuous façade.

"Of course," replied Aunt Loveday, her voice pleasant to the point of saccharine. Fractious energy waved towards me. I sensed them all, each aunt, rippling with unease but could detect nothing from Millicent, and I suspected she was using some sort of cloaking spell.

Millicent returned to the seat beside the fire and patted the sofa. "Come, dear. Sit beside me a while and tell me all about your day. I've heard what wonders you've done at the apothecary you and your aunts have set up. It's causing quite a stir in my neck of the woods, and I know several ladies who have placed orders with you. They speak glowingly about the rejuvenating creams you sell. I really must visit. I'm told it's a beautifully quaint shop with wonderful energy. It would be much appreciated if you could spare some time for the W.I. We have regular educational sessions and I'm sure our members could learn a lot from you."

My aunts glanced from one to the other, their shock barely hidden. However, her flattering words were pleasing to hear; I loved our shop and it pleased me to know that others saw it the way I did too. "We've worked hard to make it a success," I said sitting down on the sofa.

"So I have heard. It is simply marvellous what can be achieved these days, is it not, Loveday."

"Indeed," agreed Aunt Loveday. "We like to think that we're making a difference to our customers and the village."

"Oh, we are!" I said remembering the menopausally-challenged woman from this morning. "I really think that we are."

The room grew silent.

"I have also heard of your sleuthing talents."

Again the room was silent without my aunts offering comment.

"Well, there have been a few issues."

"And a fair few disasters too," Millicent said.

She continued to smile in that friendly, extremely charming way but my heart beat a little harder. Here it was. She had judged me and found me wanting. I was a delinquent witch! Would I be shipped off to the Academy? Locked up until I could be rehabilitated.

"Millicent," said Aunt Loveday, "would you be so kind as to explain what you mean by 'disasters'?"

"Certainly, Loveday. There are rumours of gossip among the covens. And then there is the incident with Vladimir Drakul – we heard that he managed to claim three more wives, transmogrify some West Highland Terriers, and terrify the village during his stay."

"It was a Pomeranian. And there was only one dog."

"People do exaggerate and make mountains out of molehills," said Aunt Beatrice with a nervous laugh.

Aunt Loveday threw Aunt Beatrice a warning glare. Millicent's charming smile didn't falter.

"Livitha has also been spotted flying through the night sky on a plastic broom." Here she laughed as though with gentle amusement but then became serious and I caught a glint of steel in her eyes. "We must live among humans without notoriety, sisters, without disrepute. We all know what happens when humans begin to fear us."

As she spoke, I sensed danger.

Aunt Thomasin drew a sharp breath. "Are you intimating that Livitha is bringing the covens into disrepute, Millicent?" She asked the question in a neutral tone although I sensed her outrage.

"Why no. Of course not, although it is always a good idea to be reminded of our place, our responsibility as such."

She did think I was delinquent. What was the punishment for that? I knew, from Aunt Beatrice's description of her job, that there was a Department for the Rehabilitation of Delinquent Witches at Hemlock Academy for Advanced Witchcraft. Would I be sent there for rehabilitation?

Sensing growing concern among my aunts, I took the initiative. They were usually so lively but had begun to resemble a clutch of waxwork dolls, their true thoughts and reactions hidden. "I apologise for any errors I may have made," I said making my best effort to sound genuine.

Millicent threw me an accepting smile. "I'm sure that you will. If not, there are ... processes in place."

Aunt Loveday's nostrils flared almost imperceptibly. Aunt Thomasin stiffened a fraction more, and Aunt Euphemia glanced from Millicent and then to me, her fixed smile dropping infinitesimally. Beside me Aunt Beatrice gripped my hand.

The sense of foreboding and doom increased. I began to feel queasy. Something was wrong, very, very wrong.

"Do you recall Katterina Blackwood, ladies?"

After a moment's silence and a slight questioning frown, Aunt Loveday replied, "Yes. I have heard of her."

"She is related to the Blackwoods in these parts, is she not?"

Aunt Loveday nodded; a flicker of concern quickly extinguished. "I do believe that she is."

"Oh, yes, she is," said Aunt Beatrice. "Maximus Blackwood, her brother, owns a large estate in Northumberland, far grander than the Blackwood estate here. They are cousins."

Millicent nodded. "And you are aware of her misdemeanour and the sentence passed by the W. I.?"

"I have not heard," stated Aunt Loveday.

"Oh, I think I know this one," said Aunt Beatrice.

A wisp of malicious enjoyment floated across Millicent's face before being replaced by the façade of sweetness. "She was found guilty, in absentia, of meddling with the dark arts."

"Oh, yes! But I think that her work-"

Millicent held up a hand. "Her work is important, I am sure-"

"Oh, it's critical!"

Millicent turned to Aunt Beatrice. "Sister, dear, may I ask that you hold your tongue."

"Indeed, I must-."

Millicent waved her hand. I felt the charge of energy as it passed me and hit Aunt Beatrice. Her mouth closed instantly and from the mumbles that followed it was clear that Millicent had cast a spell against her.

"How very dare you!" countered Aunt Loveday.

Again, Millicent raised a hand, the threat obvious. Aunt Loveday made no further comment though with lips pursed, the fixed smile had gone.

"Katterina Blackwood was a woman of great power and knowledge. That she turned to the dark arts is ... unfortunate, but it was foretold."

The hairs at the back of my neck began to creep. "If I may ask, what happened to her?"

"She was found guilty of treasonous acts and sentenced to death."

"Death!"

"Yes, death. It was the only way. Given her knowledge, exile was out of the question."

"And so, is she ... dead?"

"She is under supervision, but that day will come, yes."

Aunt Beatrice's lips pursed harder.

"And her ... turning to the dark arts was foretold?"

"Yes, it was."

Aunt Loveday drew a deep breath. "Millicent, I fail to see what this story has to do with Livitha."

"I know that you do, so I shall tell you. We have received information that difficulties lie ahead for Livitha. Difficulties that may tempt her to the dark side."

"I would never-"

Millicent's hand shot up. "That's as may be, but it is best to be forewarned."

"So, you don't want to recruit me for the Academy?"

"Of course not, you are far too immature for that."

"I'm fifty!"

"You are a child in terms of your powers. They need reigning in and controlling."

"So, you want to enrol me on your programme for delinquent witches?"

Millicent laughed in amusement. "Oh, no. We neither want to recruit you nor enrol you but we are ... watching." Her eyes locked to mine with an intense gaze.

I was under surveillance!

"Now, it has been a tremendous pleasure, but I really must be getting home. Loveday, could you tell me the best way out of here. I'm a little lost on these roads. Give me a broom and I can find a needle in a haystack, but I'm unclear on the roads I must take. They change them so often I simply cannot keep up. Ah, for simpler days."

"Indeed," replied Loveday.

"A satnav would help," I suggested.

"Yes, I daresay it would. Grimlock suggested one just the other day. Perhaps it is time I invested in one."

Murmurs of agreement.

"Now, as I was saying, it has been a pleasure to see you all again. We must do it again very soon. And, on a final note – in my professional capacity – I must ask that you report anything unusual, any strange events or occurrences, in regard to your newest acolyte." She threw me a gracious smile.

"Of course," Aunt Loveday replied.

"Come along, Loveday. The day is not getting any younger. Walk me out and give me direction." Hooking an arm through Loveday's she steered her to the door. We remained in silence as they left the room.

Chapter Six

"Insufferable!" Aunt Thomasin huffed. "The woman is simply insufferable."

"She seemed very nice ... at first," I said.

"She is a poisonous snake!" she replied. "Devious and despicable."

"She is," agreed Aunt Euphemia.

I didn't doubt my aunt's assessment but remained confused. "It was so odd. I liked her immediately but there was such a whiff of dark energy coming from her it was suffocating."

"And did you see what she did to poor Beatrice?" Aunt Euphemia asked, her face grown pallid. "Outrageous!"

"She tried to get into my mind," I said, still dazed from the experience.

"I saw that! We should raise a Protestation!"

"To whom should we protest, dear? She has everything sewn up. Her influence runs through the highest levels. Don't you recall what happened to Robart Wodewyke? He tried to protest against her, and he was exiled. I haven't seen him since."

"Poor Robart!"

The room had exploded with indignation as soon as Millicent was off Haligern land. Until that moment Loveday had instructed us to keep our counsel and only talk about the mundane and we had fallen into a stilted conversation about what we were to have for supper, which herbs needed collecting under tonight's moon and what lotions, potions, and elixirs were running low at the shop.

"If anyone has dabbled in dark magick it is her!" exclaimed Euphemia.

"Now, now," soothed Aunt Loveday. "If she found out that you were talking that way, she would have you punished."

"Malicious gossip," stated Aunt Thomasin.

"It is not. It is my opinion," insisted Aunt Euphemia.

"Yes, of course but what I meant was that she would say that it was malicious gossip," explained Aunt Thomasin. "That would be the accusation upon which you would be tried."

"It seems to me that anyone who rises up against her, or challenges her, or opposes her, is suddenly before a tribunal at the W.I." Aunt Euphemia said.

"And sentenced to death!"

"Oh, Beatrice, you have your voice back."

"Yes! And no thanks to that … that woman!" Aunt Beatrice was apoplectic. "Insufferable! Just … just insufferable."

"Now, now, dear. Let's remain calm. Sisters, I think tea is in order," Aunt Loveday suggested.

"Yes, I agree, tea always makes things better." Aunt Thomasin moved towards the sink and reached for the kettle.

"But we really must talk about what happened," said Aunt Euphemia. "Millicent's visit was a warning."

"Indeed," agreed Aunt Loveday, "but let's make tea first then we shall talk about what course of action we need to take with regard to this problem."

Four pairs of eyes sparkling with turbulent magick fell upon me. "Me? I'm the problem?"

"No!"

"Of course not, dear."

As Aunt Beatrice took over from Aunt Thomasin and busied herself preparing the tea, the conversation continued around the kitchen table.

"And we're to report Livitha if we notice any 'unusual' occurrences. By Thor's hammer but it is just unacceptable," stated Aunt Euphemia as the teapot was placed at the centre of the table.

"What does she even mean by 'unusual occurrences'? That is par for the course around here," said Aunt Thomasin beginning to pour tea into five waiting cups. "Our lives are a perpetual round of unusual occurrences.

I was about to offer up my experience with the gypsy-witch and her troubling reading of my future - which would definitely come under the category of an 'unusual occurrence' - when an inner voice told me to wait. Whether it was an ancient voice or just my instinct, I could not tell but, instead of speaking, I took a sip of tea then bit into one of Aunt Beatrice's raisin and ginger biscuits. Aunt Thomasin had insisted on adding a few drops of her calmative elixir to the teapot and quite soon the atmosphere within the kitchen had soothed a little.

Thankfully, Aunt Beatrice was so invested in complaining about Millicent's overreach in casting a spell against her that she was oblivious to my thoughts but, just to be safe, I pushed them away and began to think of Garrett instead. He had made no mention of cousins who lived in the north, and I realised that, despite our relationship growing closer in the last few months, I knew really very little about him or his family. Plus, I was yet to discover the history of the room with the heavy chair with shackles and clawed panelling. As my aunts continued to dissect the meeting and express their outrage at Millicent's abuse of power and trampling of coven etiquette, I lost myself in thoughts of Garrett. We were having dinner tomorrow and he had arranged afternoon tea at the manor with his Uncle Tobias later in the week. The thought made me nervous. The first time I had met his uncle I had thrown Alfred, Aunt Loveday's grimoire, at him. I hoped that he wouldn't be holding onto that grudge.

"So, Livitha. What do you think?"

"About what?" I asked.

"She was away with the fairies!"

"Thinking about her young man no doubt."

I nodded. "Guilty," I smiled and took another sip of tea sure that Aunt Thomasin had placed more than a few drops of her special elixir in the pot; the calm feeling I had was becoming cloudlike and I floating.

"She's had too much tea," stated Aunt Beatrice. "Just look at her eyes. The pupils are dilated."

"Well, I thought it for the best given that Millicent had assaulted her. She tried that trick with me once and I had nightmares for days afterwards."

"I still think we should raise a Protestation. It was unacceptable behaviour."

Murmurs of lacklustre agreement.

"Anyway, as I was saying ... have we agreed on what the true purpose of Millicent's visit was?" asked Aunt Euphemia.

"To spy on me," I stated. "She wants you to spy on me."

My aunts glanced between themselves.

Aunt Loveday leant across the table and placed her hand over mine. "That will not happen, my dear."

"But it's what she came for."

"Yes, Livitha, I think that you are right."

"But what could she have heard about Livitha to cause her such concern? We have not discussed that."

Again the image of the gypsy-witch pushed itself into my mind. I pushed it away and took another sip of tea—it really was delicious.

"It would have helped if she had shared that knowledge."

Murmured agreement.

"It must be something bad though."

Nods of agreement.

"Livitha, do you have any idea what it could be?"

"No," I lied. Again four pairs of eyes fell on me. "I really don't. I have no idea."

Silence filled the room.

"It is a conundrum," stated Aunt Beatrice with eyes on me. "Perhaps clarity will come soon."

"Read the tealeaves, Thomasin."

"Yes, do!"

Aunt Thomasin took my cup the moment I placed it down, swilled it round, then upturned it onto the saucer. She peered into the cup, frowned, glanced at me from beneath dark lashes, then replaced it. "I see nothing," she stated. "It must be the stress from Millicent's visit."

"Yes, perhaps so," agreed Aunt Loveday, a slight frown quickly smoothing.

Aunt Euphemia sighed in disappointment. "I just hope that that is the last we shall see of Millicent for the rest of this year."

"I hope that she breaks down on the way home."

"I directed her across Wolfstane Moor!"

All eyes turned to Aunt Loveday.

"What?" she asked, unable to keep a smile from the corner of her mouth. "It was the shortest route."

Aunt Beatrice snickered, Aunt Thomasin snorted, Aunt Euphemia gasped and then all four began to cackle.

"Oh, Loveday, you always did have a wicked sense of humour!"

Chapter Seven

The following morning I woke unrefreshed and with a sense of impending doom but hoped that my dinner tonight with Garrett would help fix it. My thoughts wandered to his Uncle Tobias and the afternoon tea I had been invited to. My stomach flipped. Inviting me home to meet his uncle was like being asked to meet a lover's mother—it was the next stage in formalising our relationship. One day, I hoped, I'd be able to bring Garrett home to meet my aunts. Obviously, they knew him, but arranging high tea, or even more seriously, dinner, would be the next stage in their acceptance of him. I tried to suppress my unease, blaming it on the peculiar meeting with the gypsy-witch and then Millicent's ominous warning. I showered, pulled on my dressing gown, then checked my face for unwanted facial hair. After plucking several hairs from my top lip I spotted one growing from my chin!

Apart from the erratic hormones and the hot sweats, hairs sprouting on my face was the worst side effect of the dreaded 'change' and it seemed grossly unfair that my aunts seemed not to have suffered this challenge to their womanly attractions.

"Well!" I exclaimed as I tugged at the offending hair. "This is going to have to go."

"Yes, it is rather repellent," the acerbic voice rose from beside my feet.

"Lucifer! You startled me. Whatever are you doing in my bathroom?"

Lucifer ignored my reprimand and jumped up onto the vanity unit, studying my reflection in the mirror. "There's more than one."

"More than one what?"

"Hair. More than one long, white, and wiry hair. Ugh. I have to say Mistress Erickson, that growing a beard really will not suit you. You should perhaps give up on the idea."

"I'm not trying to grow a beard!" Despite growing used to Lucifer's acerbic comments he always managed to hit a sore point—a malicious intuition that he revelled in. Horrid cat!

"I'm getting rather a whiff of bad energy coming from you, Livitha."

"I wonder why."

"Well, I am only trying to help. Growing a beard really won't do you any favours. It is bad enough that you have a moustache-"

"I do not!" I threw him a glare. He was not helping my already fractious energy.

"I doubt Master Blackwood would enjoy having a wife with facial hair as thick as his own. Men tend not to like such things. They see it ... well, some could see it as a challenge to their manliness-"

"Lucifer!"

"Whilst others would find it repellent."

"My facial hair is not a challenge to Garrett's manliness! Have you been at Aunt Euphemia's elixir again? You're not making sense."

He snorted. "Don't blame the messenger." He raised a paw and licked at it whilst watching me in the mirror.

I returned to my reflection. I really couldn't see the other hair or hairs he was referring to so pushed the curtains back to let more light into the room and peered closer to the glass.

"You're just being mean, Lucifer. There are no more hairs on my chin."

"There are. There's quite a gathering of them. Perhaps you are becoming a man?"

His tone was sincere.

"Of course I'm not turning into a man! I'm ... it's just hormones."

"Yes, testosterone."

"Lucifer, did you just come up here to annoy me? If I promise you some salmon, will you go away?"

"How rude!"

"That is the pot calling the kettle black." I turned my head and raised my chin hoping to cast better light beneath it. Still, there was nothing to be seen.

"Perhaps spectacles would help?"

"I don't need glasses, Lucifer. I'm not that old!"

"Well, I can clearly see hairs. There's practically a shrub sprouting from your chin." He snorted, his shoulders heaving, and I realised that he was teasing me.

"Okay, the joke is over. Now, if you would be so kind, I need to finish my toilette."

"Yes, and hurry, the aunts want to speak to you."

"Is that what you came here to tell me?"

"It is."

"Did they ask you to come and fetch me?"

"They did." He jumped down from the vanity unit.

"Did they say what for?"

"They did not." He flicked his tail and strolled out of the bathroom with regal disdain.

The knot in my stomach twisted; my aunts never sent for me this early in the morning and I wasn't late for breakfast.

I made my way downstairs, stomach churning, the tips of my fingers fizzing, and stepped into the kitchen. A hush fell among my aunts, the air crackled with fractious energy, and the fizzing turned to sparks.

"She's very anxious," said Aunt Euphemia as I walked across the room.

"Lucifer said that you wanted to speak to me."

"Ah, yes, well, sit down first and have a cup of tea," said Aunt Thomasin. Her usual relaxed manner had been replaced by a concerned frown and she seemed tired.

I sat down feeling like a child about to be given a lecture for some misdemeanour, the gypsy-witch's warning repeating in my mind and melding with Millicent's, but I quickly turned my thoughts to Garrett and his Uncle Tobias; I couldn't let Aunt Beatrice know about the doom-laden prophecy.

Had Lucifer said 'husband'? He had!

Aunt Beatrice wafted the air as she placed a cup and saucer on the table. "She is definitely anxious, but I can't say I blame her. Afternoon tea with Tobias Blackwood would make anybody nervous."

"Livitha, is this true? Are you to have afternoon tea with Tobias Blackwood?"

I nodded. "Yes, Garrett has asked me to meet his uncle. He wants us to get to know one another."

"Just try not to kill him this time, dear," said Aunt Euphemia with a glint in her eyes. "Then I'm sure all will be well."

Aunt Thomasin laughed and then Aunt Beatrice giggled. The tension broke.

"Tobias Blackwood! Ah, sisters, do you remember-"

"Now is not the time for that."

"Oh, but he was so handsome!"

"And look where that got him. Banished and stripped of his powers."

"Well, he really shouldn't have played with fire. Adriana and Bertha were always rivals. He should have chosen one as his mate and not pitted them one against the other."

"True."

The atmosphere in the room relaxed and my fingers, though still painful at the tips, no longer crackled or fizzed.

"I just hope he likes me," I said.

"Pah! What's not to like, dear. You will be fine. And to be honest, Garrett Blackwood is a far better catch than Pascal Carlton."

"She won't be able to turn a Blackwood into a frog with quite such ease though."

"I don't want to!"

"Pascal was a philandering toad, he deserved it."

"I doubt he thought that."

"Are you defending him?"

"No, of course not."

"He was a philandering toad, an adulterous miscreant."

"Indeed, we can all agree on that."

"It is just a shame that Livitha clung onto the marriage for so long."

"Do you mind? I am still in the room."

"Well, it is true."

"Sisters, perhaps we can dissect Livitha's disastrous marriage another time. This morning we have an important task."

"It wasn't disastrous!" My protestation went unnoticed.

"Oh, yes, of course—the task."

I sipped the tea poured by Aunt Beatrice, hoping that they had secretly dropped in some of Aunt Thomasin's calming elixir, and waited.

Breakfast continued and the kettle was filled with water to freshen the pot but explanations as to the 'important task' were not forthcoming. I took a second slice of Aunt Beatrice's toasted bread and lathered it with butter then marmalade, nerves beginning to fray.

With a final sip of her tea, Aunt Loveday sat up in her chair and placed the bone china cup in its saucer. The signal was picked up by my aunts and they all turned to her.

"Livitha."

"Yes?"

"We have been remiss in your education."

"Oh?"

"In other words, we have failed you."

"Oh, no! I'm sure that's not true. How can you have failed me?"

"Well, the last months have been like riding the Atlantic in a storm—so many troughs and peaks among the waves that it has been all but impossible to find a quiet moment for instruction. However, there have been times where I could have imparted knowledge, and I have not taken them as readily as I should have."

"But you have been unwell, Loveday. Let's not forget that," said Aunt Euphemia.

"And Livitha is not the Titanic!" added Aunt Beatrice. "Despite hitting a few enormous icebergs," she formed a large circle with her arms, "she is still afloat."

My aunts nodded.

"Thanks!"

"And it would have been impossible to carry out instruction with you in such a state."

Aunt Loveday nodded. "Thank you, sisters. Yes, I agree though I do feel that I have shirked my responsibilities-"

Aunt Thomasin sat forward. "Now, Loveday! I really must take you to task there. You have never shirked your responsibilities. The fact is that Liv coming into her power coincided with numerous unfortunate events."

"Icebergs!"

"Yes, and let's also not forget that those events were opportunities for learning, and I am certain that Liv gained much from the experiences she has endured."

Aunt Loveday sighed. "You are right, sisters."

"You must not be so harsh upon yourself, Loveday. No other could have done more than yourself—under the circumstances."

Again she nodded although the serious countenance remained unchanged. "That may very well be true, but it does not change the fact that Livitha's instruction is woefully behind and after Millicent's visit yesterday it is obvious that we are at a critical juncture. She must be fortified against whatever the future holds, whatever opportunities arise to test her, and whatever journey she must endure. So, it is time—before it is too late."

"Before she hits an enormous iceberg that tears into her hull, and she sinks like a stone to the darkest depths of the freezing Atlantic Ocean." Aunt Beatrice gave a dramatic shudder.

"Yes, thank you, Beatrice."

The knot in my stomach tightened.

"I agree."

"So do I."

Four pairs of eyes rested on me.

"So, Livitha, this morning Euphemia will take your place at the shop, and you will work with me. It is time to begin your instruction in the art of magick, and in earnest. There is no time to delay."

Chapter Eight

We stood in the field behind the vegetable garden. In the corner, the two cursed goats stood watching from the doorway of their pen. Aunt Loveday's wolfhound familiar, Renweard, sat by her side watching the plumes of smoke rise from the crab apple tree at the bottom of the field.

"Do we have to do it here?" I asked. "Old Mawde and Hegelina Fekket are staring at me. It's off-putting," I complained.

"No, this is where we have to work. We need a wide-open space. Now, remember to focus on each finger. The energy travels down each of them individually so unfocused energy can be problematic but when you are proficient, you will be able to use each one separately, or at least each hand independent of the other; it is quite within your reach—if you learn to focus."

"That would be amazing," I said staring at my hands and then glancing at the scorched tree in the distance. Small fires had set within the grass and Aunt Thomasin batted at them with a broom.

"Your hands are very powerful, Livitha. Weapons of destruction and manipulation. Each finger acts as a wand, a conductor of magic."

"Wouldn't it be easier to have a wand?" I asked.

Aunt Loveday sucked in a breath and her eyes flickered with disapproval. "Wands are for warlocks and wizards, dear, not witches. And before you start to say that that is sexist or some other new-fangled nonsense, it is not. Warlocks and wizards do not have the power to use their own fingers as conductors, they need to use wands in order to channel their magick. It is just the way it is. And being able to use each hand independently gives our power much more flexibility. They have one wand whilst we have ten fingers! Granted, that brings its own problems, but when a witch masters the art there really is no comparison."

"Oh, I see."

"Good, now let us focus. And this time, try to hit the target. And let's not have any peonies on the oak tree again, marvellous as that was. You must learn to contain your power rather than give it free reign."

I glanced at the tree burning at the end of the field. Aunt Loveday was being kind by not mentioning the destruction my attempts at throwing out my energies had just caused, referring instead to the time I had exploded with uncontrolled magick and caused the oak tree to burst into peony-like blossom.

"At this point, I just want to make sure I don't set myself on fire! I have such tingling in my fingers and they keep sparking when I get anxious. I nearly set my hair on fire at the shop last month and my bedsheets have singe holes in them!"

Aunt Loveday eyed me with concern. "Yes, that would never do. A bald witch is not a pretty sight."

"She has a beard to balance it out though."

"Lucifer! What are you doing here?"

"Watching."

"You'll put me off."

"Then I shall enjoy watching you fail."

"Lucifer!" scolded Aunt Loveday. "Livitha is not going to fail! You may not be in a good mood, but that is no excuse to be rude."

"It's her fault."

"How can it be my fault?"

"It just is," he sulked.

I had no idea what I had done to offend Lucifer, but he was taking umbrage at something. "Can't we send him home, please?"

"Let him stay. His presence will help give you practice in not giving in to distraction." She turned to the vicious feline. "Now, Lucifer, behave yourself."

"He's just attention seeking."

The cat sat in regal disdain with eyes closed. "Go ahead. Don't mind me."

"We won't."

"Now Livitha, remember that you must remain centred. Centre your energy. Focus your mind. Embrace the ancient knowledge our ancestors have granted you."

I nodded and took a fighting stance.

"Very ladylike!"

"Ignore him."

I ignored him.

Placing my feet at hip distance apart, a stance that Aunt Loveday assured would help me cope with the kick back, I pushed the sleeves of my fleece to my elbows, then focused my energy, imagining it flowing from the core of my being, up through my torso, to my shoulders, down my arms, and out through each of my fingers.

"There's a beast on Wolfstane Moor."

A flash of sparks erupted from the tips of my fingers, and began to whirl, sparkling like a Catherine Wheel firework. A clump of grass less than twenty feet away began to smoulder.

"Oh," said Aunt Loveday.

Lucifer chuckled.

"That was not fair!" I complained.

"You'll thank me one day," he replied without any hint of remorse.

"You must focus, Livitha, no matter what else is happening around you. Now, again. Try again."

Once again, I focused on the circular target at the end of the field.

"Aim for the centre. Thomasin, make way!"

Aunt Thomasin scurried behind us, and I focused my energy whilst keeping the black circle at the centre of the straw target in sight. Energy burst from my fingertips, the force of its eruption making me take a step back."

"They do say that the beast is a Blackwood," Lucifer stated dryly.

The current of energy from my fingers arced and I lost control. Flashes and sparks fizzed. The flow of energy buckled and then divided into ten separate lines of current hitting the ground then ricocheting upwards.

"Livitha!"

"I can't stop it!" I yelled as the flow of energy grew more intense.

The beast was a Blackwood!

Garrett was the monster!

The room at the Manor was for him!

Magical energy as bright as a bolt of lightning scorched the grass. I swung away from Aunt Loveday just as she created a protective shield around her, Lucifer, Renweard, and Aunt Thomasin. A bolt of bucking erratic energy hit her shield, bounced off and travelled towards the goat pen where Old Mawde and Hegelina Fekkit stood watching. The bolt landed between them. Both jerked as though doing a St. Vitus dance and then, with hides smouldering, they bleated and galloped from the pen.

"Turn it off!" commanded Aunt Loveday.

The shock of hitting the cursed goats refocused my mind and the crackling energy subdued to sparks then died.

Old Mawde and Hegelina Fekkit stood watching me from the opposite side of the field. Both bleated their disapproval. Aunt Loveday's iridescent protective shield disappeared.

"Well," she said whilst catching her breath, "I think we'll finish here for today."

"I'm sorry," I gasped. "I'm so sorry."

"Not to worry. No real harm done, but you really must focus. You've done very well ... all things considered." She cast a disapproving glance at Lucifer.

The cursed goats continued to bleat.

"Will they be alright?" I asked.

"Oh, yes," replied Aunt Loveday. "They're full of condemnation but forget why they are themselves cursed. They've been rebellious of late; I think this will remind them of our powers." She smiled and waved to the bleating goats. They turned to each other then turned their backs to us. "Silly old hags," she muttered.

"Lucifer was right. I've failed."

"Nonsense," she said and took hold of my hands. "These are weapons, Livitha. Very powerful weapons. You just need to learn how to focus. It takes time but you will succeed."

Her words were soothing although I doubted my ability to get the 'weapons' under control.

"Tomorrow we will practice levitation. Something small and light to begin with, I think. And try this again next week."

I eyed Lucifer. "I can't wait. Perhaps I should try practicing tonight? I could practice on Lucifer, he's small and light."

Lucifer hissed then disappeared leaving a cloud of black hairs in his wake.

Chapter Nine

We made our way back to the cottage where Aunt Beatrice and Euphemia listened to the tale of my disastrous training session. Both were laughing.

"It was the funniest thing I've seen in an age," laughed Aunt Thomasin. "Did you see Old Mawde buck?"

"Well, they had it coming," said Aunt Loveday without compassion.

"It's true," agreed Aunt Thomasin. "They have been beastly this last few days. Very restless."

"That means there's trouble brewing. You know what they say about cursed goats."

"No, Beatrice, enlighten me. What do they say about cursed goats?"

"I don't remember exactly, but it is something along the lines of ... 'Listen to cursed goats when they are p ... ahem ... angry, for they portend of dreadful days that shall not be missed."

"You're making it up!"

"And badly, too!"

"No, I'm not. Goats, particularly of the cursed variety, are extremely sensitive to changes in the magical atmosphere. Do you not remember that time when Camilla de Vetch was colluding with Hegelina Fekkit to steal Old Man Dobson's woodlands? They wanted to use the burial mounds for their dark magick rituals."

Aunt Loveday shuddered. "Yes! If they had been successful, then ... it just doesn't bear thinking about."

"Indeed, and Old Mawde had been vile that week. She was the first to sense it and it is thanks to her that their plans were thwarted."

"Just how long has Old Mawde been cursed for?" I asked.

"Oh, quite some time."

"Yes, but how long?"

"Since the time of the last Queen of England," Aunt Loveday spoke rapidly and turned her head away.

"Elizabeth the first?"

"No! We're not monsters! Anne. She was the last queen, before the Union."

My history was rusty, but I knew that Queen Anne had come to the throne during the early eighteenth century. "But that's ... that's more than three hundred years!"

"It is."

"Don't you think that perhaps she could be released now? I mean, three hundred years is a long time."

"Pah! Not long enough for what she did."

"What did she do exactly?"

My aunts glanced one to the other. "She colluded with an enemy. She brought disrepute to the coven."

"It caused us so much pain," Aunt Thomasin sighed. "She had been a good sister until then."

"Pah! She was a wolf hiding in sheep's clothing, Thomasin. Why, she always was the first to cause trouble. Always wanting to dig into the dark side of magick."

"She loved adventure though and was very passionate."

"Hah, yes! And look where that got her."

"Was she family?" I asked, more curious about the woman who had been turned into a goat three centuries ago and was still living at the bottom of our garden.

Aunt Loveday pursed her lips though her eyes flickered with pain.

"She was, Livitha, yes."

"It is a torment when a sister goes bad. Truly."

"And what was it that she did?"

Aunt Loveday took a deep breath. "Well, there was collusion, but what finally did it ... is Euphemia's story, really, but ... Mawde was a great beauty and charismatic with it. She knew just how to get you to do what she wanted."

"And she had a streak of evil so thick that if you cut her in half, it would be written there. E. V. I. L." said Aunt Beatrice tracing the letters across her stomach, "just as though she were a stick of rock, like the ones you can purchase at the seaside. Usually, they have Blackpool or Skegness written through—very clever. Really quite mind-boggling when you think about it."

"Yes, very interesting and ... graphic, dear."

"And true!"

"Yes, and true. We're not denying that."

"So, did she practice the dark arts? Is that why she was cursed?"

"She did."

"And the punishment is exile or death!" Aunt Beatrice said with exaggeration. "But we saved her."

I glanced out of the window. The two goats were butting horns. Old Mawde had a dark patch on her rump where my magick had singed her coat. "Is three hundred years as a goat really worse than death? Why didn't she go into exile? That's where Hegelina was."

"Well, that was Euphemia's doing."

"She saved her from death?"

My aunts exchanged glances. "Well ... you could put it that way."

"It was a kindness—living as a cursed goat or death. No competition really."

"What did she do, exactly?"

"She used her dark arts to steal Aunt Euphemia's fiancé. She had always been jealous of Euphemia. Always accused her of being the favourite among us and when she met and fell in love with Joaquin and he returned that love, Mawde became consumed by jealousy."

"Oh, he was so handsome! You would have thought so too, Livitha. Smouldering dark eyes with the longest lashes and dark hair, oh, such glossy dark hair, and that smile!" Aunt Beatrice sighed. "So mysterious! He was foreign you know. Came over with the Spanish Armada, got washed up ashore, and decided to stay."

"Oh?"

"Beatrice!" Aunt Loveday shot her a warning look.

"Sorry, Loveday, but you must admit he was handsome."

"Yes, I admit it, he was handsome."

"And he didn't come over on the Armada!" Aunt Thomasin corrected. "He was washed ashore, yes, but the Armada was centuries before that."

"Well, who was it that came across on the Armada? There was definitely someone." Aunt Beatrice looked pensive. "No! I cannot remember."

"It was Garcia."

"Of course it was. Euphemia was keen on him too."

"More than keen," laughed Aunt Thomasin. "She does like her men dark and handsome."

"Oh, and smouldering," added Aunt Beatrice.

Aunt Loveday sighed. "Sisters, can we get back to Old Mawde and Joaquin?"

"Yes, of course," replied Aunt Beatrice. "Ah, I do love it when memories return. It is like visiting an old and fascinating friend."

"Indeed," agreed Aunt Loveday with an indulgent smile.

"The thing is," continued Aunt Beatrice, "that Mawde just couldn't stand to see Joaquin with another woman—she'd fallen head over heels for him you see. Cupid had shot his arrow-"

"Bea!"

"Oh, yes, sorry, Loveday."

Aunt Loveday continued the story. "So, Old Mawde was terribly jealous of the pair and tried so hard to spoil their relationship but when their marriage was announced she became apoplectic."

"I remember it well," said Aunt Beatrice. "I think there are still scratches in the plaster where she clawed at the wall."

I glanced again out of the window. Old Mawde and Hegelina Fekkit stood with horns locked, neither appeared willing to concede.

"Did she stop the marriage?"

"She did."

"How?"

"She stole Joaquin from Euphemia?"

"He came here one night, and it *was* dark and stormy!" Aunt Beatrice spoke with foreboding. "On horseback! He broke down the door and demanded that Mawde be handed over to him."

"Mawde be handed over?"

"Oh, yes, and she was grinning like a Cheshire cat!"

"It was nauseating!"

"Poor Euphemia cried for days."

"So, she cast a spell on him? A dark magick spell?" I asked.

"She used her beauty to seduce him, yes."

"But that's not casting a spell ..."

"Well, no, but we're sure she did."

"Joaquin would never have abandoned Euphemia without a spell being cast."

"Although Mawde was very beautiful," added Aunt Thomasin.

"Oh, yes, and funny," said Aunt Beatrice. "She was such a card! You would have laughed, Livitha. She kept us amused-" Aunt Beatrice stopped mid-sentence as she caught Aunt Loveday's disapproving frown. "Well ... she would," she finished.

I began to wonder if Old Mawde had really used dark magick to seduce Joaquin or whether she had just used her womanly wiles on him. Men, I knew to my chagrin, were fickle.

"Why did he break down the door and demand to see Mawde?" I asked, now intrigued by the story.

"Well, Loveday had gotten word that he had fallen in love with Mawde. Euphemia was unaware although if memory serves-"

"It would have brought disrepute on the coven, for one sister to deceive another and Mawde had already caused us so much harm. I had to stop them."

"You knew they wanted to elope?"

A flush had appeared on Aunt Loveday's cheeks. "Yes," she admitted. "I couldn't allow it."

"So, you're not sure if she used dark magick?"

"She did. She admitted it—at least she did for her previous misdemeanour."

"We couldn't let the W. I. know. They would have exiled her or sentenced her to death. We could not let that shame befall us."

"So you cursed her instead?"

Aunt Loveday nodded. "She was becoming ..."

"Delinquent," Aunt Beatrice suggested. "Gone rogue!" she said with dramatic flair.

"And she's been a goat for three hundred years?"

"She has."

"Isn't that long enough? I mean ... what she did was awful, but no one died."

"Pah! Young people today! They have no sense of morality."

"But Joaquin did die. He was so heartbroken that the object of his obsession was lost to him that he pined away."

"That's sugar-coating it, Thomasin. He became a drunk and died in a brawl in the middle of the town covered in mud and straw."

"That's terrible."

"It's the consequence of using dark magick. If Old Mawde had left him alone, then he would have married Euphemia and lived happily ever after!" Aunt Loveday stated. "Just as Raif and I have done these past centuries."

So now the truth was out. To save themselves from shame, my aunts had cursed one of their own, forcing her to live as a goat at the bottom of the garden. I'd had hints of their ruthlessness before, but the depths of it were becoming clear. My aunts were wonderful. They were kind and loving. They were a wealth of knowledge and worked hard to help others. But there was a darker side to them too, one steeped in centuries of lore, tradition, and simply shaped from surviving through the changing, and often dangerous, centuries.

"Now, Livitha, we must continue your instruction. If you will fetch your grimoire, we can make some new entries."

"Oh! How wonderful!" Aunt Beatrice rubbed her hands. "I shall put the kettle on. I have several hexes that I would like to share. You will love them, Livitha. They are so ... so wicked!"

"Wicked?"

"I mean fun."

As Aunt Beatrice turned to the stove to collect the kettle, Mrs. Driscoll stepped into the room. "I've had to rearrange my hours so I'll work this afternoon instead of tomorrow morning, but I can't be long. There's a meeting at the village hall I want to go to."

Attending a Parish meeting was the last thing I'd want to do and knew that Mrs. Driscoll wasn't particularly interested in village politics either. "Oh? Something special?" I asked.

"Well, there's been another murder on the moors-"

"No!"

"Yes. And the village are up in arms about it. There's been no mention of the murders on the telly or the radio or in the papers. We want to know why people aren't being warned there's a maniac on the loose."

It was unusual for murders, particularly ones so dramatic, not to go reported in the media. "It is odd."

"Yes, it is. I think your young man has a lot of questions to answer," she stated.

"Garrett?"

"Yes. He's going to be there to talk to the community apparently."

After confirming the time of the meeting, I decided to go. The remainder of the afternoon was spent in the kitchen at the table with a perpetually refreshed pot of tea and never-ending supply of homemade biscuits and four grimoires open and pawed through.

Aunt Loveday's was the largest, thickest, and oldest, but Aunt Euphemia's was almost as large. Aunt Beatrice's was much smaller although just as thick. It was fascinating to compare them. Each contained more spells, charms, and hexes than could be counted and each had numerous pages that appeared empty to me, but which were crammed with writing hidden by magick. I made the mistake of asking Aunt Thomasin what was written on one of her empty pages and received a disapproving frown in return. "We do not ask what lies beneath the cloak of secrecy," she returned in hushed tones.

Aunt Beatrice cackled. "Take no notice of her, it's just the fruit loaf recipe that she refuses to let me have."

"Pah!"

Another cackle. "Yes, she's jealous of it! She knows that I will bake it far better than she."

"Pah!" Aunt Thomasin repeated and took a bite of one of Aunt Beatrice's biscuits. It snapped against her teeth. "It is more like I would not want you to butcher it, as you have with these biscuits."

"There is nothing wrong with my biscuits!"

"They are jaw breakers, Bea."

Aunt Beatrice sniffed. "I forgot the secret ingredient, that's all."

Aunt Loveday chuckled as they continued to spar, trading light-hearted insults, as she searched Arthur for a suitable spell to pass on to me. "So, Livitha. Do you have anything that you can add to your grimoire? We have each given you one this afternoon, but do you not have anything that instinct has delivered?"

"Do you mean from the voices?"

She nodded.

"Well, I think that perhaps I do," I said remembering the words that had been repeating in my dreams over the past weeks. The words intruded during my waking hours too. "There's something they keep repeating. I dream of it and hear it during the day—generally when I'm taking a walk."

"A classic time for them to impart knowledge."

"They catch me when I'm washing up!" said Aunt Beatrice. "Oh, we do have some nice chats."

Aunt Loveday smiled. "For me it's usually in a quiet moment."

"Well, it would be pointless at any other time. Imagine if they started talking whilst you were paying for groceries, or chatting with Mrs. Driscoll, or hoovering. It just wouldn't work."

Aunt Loveday nodded. "Quite right, Beatrice. So," she said turning her attention back to me. "The ancient voices are beginning to share their wisdom with you, and you must capture those words and arrange them in what you perceive to be the most powerful form."

"Can't I just write them down as they come?"

"Indeed, you can, but you have your own powers. Think of it like a rue. A rue is bland until the magic ingredient is added. You add the magick ingredient."

"Ah, I see. And how do I know what magick ingredient to add."

"Trial and error, intuition, research, and learning. There are many ways."

"Just don't ask for help," Aunt Thomasin said in ominous tones.

"Oh, no. Do not ask for help," agreed Beatrice.

"Why?"

"Because you don't know who will answer. There are many out there who wish us harm or want to recruit us to their side—the dark side."

"Thomasin is correct. You must listen. Do not seek."

"Old Mawde sought and look where that got her!"

"It took her to the dark side!" stated Aunt Beatrice in a lowered voice and a dramatic glance my way.

Chapter Ten

The village meeting was scheduled for seven and at eight I was to meet Garrett for dinner and, though exhausted after my training day, I showered, checked my chin and upper lip for sprouting hairs, realised I was becoming paranoid about the pesky protrusions, and got ready to go out. We were to eat at our favourite restaurant, the *Imaginarium*. Garrett had apologised for not picking me up but as he was officially 'on call' and he didn't want to leave me stranded at the restaurant if called out, we had agreed to meet there.

With half an hour to spare, I managed to sneak past Lucifer now curled up asleep on my bed and made my way downstairs. I planned to relax in the kitchen, sit by the fire, and perhaps read through my grimoire. I had only managed to fill a couple of pages with charms, several spells, and one hex, and wanted to commit them to memory. My aunts' knowledge was deep and inspiring, and I hoped to be as capable as them one day, but for now I was a witch with trainer wheels on.

The kitchen was empty, and my aunts were busy or relaxing in various rooms around the house. Ominously, Aunt Loveday had mentioned something about Vlad, our blood-sucking and difficult summer guest, returning during the New Year and was busy replying to a letter she had received yesterday. Vlad's visit had been interesting to say the least, but I had come to like the man and we had grown close. I could cope with another visit from the sunlight deprived creature, but not if he was going to bring his dog—a designer pooch bitten by his newly dead and delinquent wives and transmogrified into a canine vampire.

I sat on the tall-backed grandfather chair and placed a log on the fire, opened my grimoire and grew still. All noise ceased, even the loud ticking of the clock in the hallway disappeared. The room grew dark around me, and the table, chairs, windows, and sink disappeared. Only the orange glow from the fire remained. A vibration from my book was felt through my thighs and then letters began to peel from the page, each black letter separating from the vellum until it began to float. Spellbound and enveloped by a sensation of being wrapped in cottonwool I watched as the letters danced. They undulated like tissue on a soft breeze then reformed. I read them aloud as they settled.

"Upon the moor his heart will beat.

Upon the hearth his blood will seep.

The Beast will fall, and you will weep.

The Blackwood Curse is yours to keep."

The words fell back to the grimoire, anchoring themselves to the page as though they had never lifted. The darkness began to fade, and brightness returned to the room.

"Livitha!"

I gasped, surprised by the loudness of Aunt Loveday's voice beside me. I clapped the grimoire shut.

"Are you alright? I've been calling to you."

"Sorry!" Dazed and unsure of what had just happened, I stared down at the grimoire. My hands trembled.

"Liv?"

"Sorry," I repeated, gathering my senses. "I was deep in thought."

"Are the charms bothering you? Is the hex ... too strong?"

"Oh, no. It's not that, I was engrossed in learning them, that's all." Lying to my aunt felt wrong, but I knew this was something I had to keep from her.

"Well, if you're sure?"

"I'm sure."

"Good, then there's something we'd like to give you."

"Oh?" I realised then that my aunt was not alone, the others stood behind her, looking down at me with a mix of concern and excitement. "If it's another charm, I can write it down now."

"No, it's not a charm."

"Nor a hex."

"But it is magick!" Aunt Beatrice was breathless with excitement. "And very special."

Aunt Loveday pulled out an arm from behind her back. In her open palm was a wrap of soft leather tooled with intricate designs, similar to the beasts, birds, snakes, and wolves that populated the front of her grimoire. It was secured with a leather thong threaded with silver beads decorated with tiny runes.

"Oh! What is it?"

"Take it and see."

"Open it!"

I took the parcel from her hand and was overcome by a wave of energy. It was at once fractious and chaotic but jubilant and powerful, flexing.

"It's moving!"

Although the parcel sat on my hand without visibly moving, I could sense its kinetic energy, barely contained.

"Open it and see!"

I placed the parcel on my knee and tugged at the thong. It loosened then fell away and I opened the parcel to reveal a wide silver bangle. "It's just like yours," I said holding it in the flat of my palm, admiring the workmanship wrought into its surface. My earliest memories were of my aunts' silver bangles and as a child I would often try to touch them, fascinated by the coiled and intertwined beasts moulded there.

"It's similar, but not exactly the same. They're all different. Each has its unique character."

"They're moving!"

"They do move, but it's if they step off the bangle that you need to be a little more concerned."

"If they step off the bangle!"

"Now, don't be dramatic, dear. It's another one of those elements of our lives that you will learn to understand."

"I agree, it is rather ... unsettling at first, although you will grow to appreciate them rather quickly, I think."

"Definitely. In the current climate."

"You're not making this any easier. Do you mean to tell me that these – I scrutinised the creatures on the bangle – that these snakes and worms will come to life, and I should be grateful?"

"No, no, no! Oh, dear. We have been remiss. No, they are definitely not snakes and worms!"

"They look like snakes or worms!"

"Tsk! They are wild boars, dragons, snakes, wolves—all the wonderful creatures we have embraced over the centuries."

"And they come alive?"

"At times, yes."

"At what times?"

"Well, generally we try to make sure they stay put."

"But?"

"But sometimes, they do ... shift a little."

"When exactly do they shift?"

"Well, it's when there's a problem."

"But there have been plenty of problems recently and I haven't seen them move or jump off your bands."

"Well, it's when there's a serious problem." Aunt Euphemia avoided my gaze.

"What Euphemia is trying to say is that the creatures come alive when there is an existential threat to the coven."

"Yes, they're a warning system if you like. Guardians of sorts"

"Hah!" interjected Aunt Thomasin, "Of sorts is correct."

"Yes, they do get it wrong sometimes."

"I don't think it's a matter of them getting it wrong. They are intricately woven with our own psyche, so if a witch is deficient somehow ... then they are impeded in their job."

"Oh, yes, do you remember Jocelyn of Wattlington?"

Aunt Beatrice groaned.

"Ah yes. That was a disaster."

"Disaster is an understatement; the fire dragon burned her to a crisp."

Examining the intertwined animals on my own bangle, I could discern at least three heads. "Yours are a bird, a boar, and a dragon, dear," explained Loveday. "So lucky!"

"Lucky! There's a dragon on my bangle and you've just told me that one burned a witch to a crisp because she was 'deficient'!" I was definitely deficient!

"Well, when I said deficient, I meant-"

"Delinquent!" interrupted Aunt Beatrice.

"Oh, Beatrice, not every witch is delinquent. Since you've taken that post at the Academy, your worldview has certainly shifted."

"It has opened my eyes, dear. That is all. I'm just far more aware of how precarious our situation is. Delinquent witches are a serious problem. And the way society is going, they're becoming more prolific."

Aunt Loveday sighed.

Aunt Thomasin rolled her eyes. "Very good, Bea."

"I have to say that you're becoming a little too obsessed with this new job."

"It's fascinating!" Aunt Beatrice's eyes glittered. "And so exciting!"

"Is this why she has been acting 'off' recently?"

Aunt Loveday nodded.

"It's all Grimlock's fault," Aunt Thomasin added. "He's the one who suggested her for the post."

"And I'm glad that he did. I haven't had so much fun in decades. Centuries, even," Aunt Beatrice exclaimed, defiant eyes glittering.

"Well, I'm glad that you're having so much fun, Beatrice." Aunt Thomasin sipped her tea whilst looking out of the window, further commentary held back.

"Talking of fun ... isn't it time for the village meeting?"

"It is!"

I kissed each of my aunts, thanking them for the beautiful though terrifying gift, and left Haligern for my first Parish meeting. I hoped it would be my last.

Chapter Eleven

They do say that the Beast of Wolfstane Moor is a Blackwood.

Lucifer's words repeated in my mind and as I drove through the winding lanes, the nearly full moon bright in the night sky, I grew increasingly anxious, my palms sweating. The bangle glinted in the moonlight and more than once I thought that the fire dragon's coiled tail had flexed. The movement was caught in the corner of my eye but when I glanced at it directly it remained perfectly still. My fingers fizzed. The knot in my stomach began to heat. "Keep it calm, Erickson," I murmured as I reached the peak of the final hill before entering the village. Streetlights glowed in the distance.

Outside the village hall, a surprisingly large throng of people surrounded the entrance and I had to drive past the building and then turn down another street to find a parking spot. Mrs. Driscoll hadn't exaggerated when she said that the murders were the talk of the village. I parked then walked to the village hall and joined the queue of people as they waited to go inside. The night had turned chilly and, dressed for the restaurant, I didn't have my usual layers on to fend off the cold. Thankfully, the cluster of people thinned quickly, and I didn't have long to wait. Warm air hit me as I entered, the heater above the doors on full blast.

The rows of chairs set out to face the table at the far end of the room were already full, leaving standing room only and my view was blocked by several men, all far taller and broader than me. I spent several minutes slipping between them to the back row of seating where I would be able to see.

The room was filled with villagers, many talking, some silent, arms held defensively across their chests. The atmosphere was belligerent.

As a side door at the front of the room opened, the chatter subsided then fell to a hush. Garrett, accompanied by a female colleague and a woman I recognised as Karyn Montpellier née Idle, the classmate who was now a local dignitary, and wife of the man who had visited my shop, made their way to the table. I also recognised her as the runner who had jogged past me close to the site of the gypsy's caravans.

The women sat whilst Garrett remained standing. I hated public speaking, but Garrett didn't seem phased at all. His confidence was one of the things I loved about him but then, if you were a werewolf, maybe that came with the territory; whoever heard of an alpha male shapeshifter with a confidence problem? My mind travelled to the films I'd watched. The cursed men were haunted, conflicted by their desires, but never nervous, anxious, or timorous. And they were never weak! No, they were strong and muscular with strong jawlines and broad shoulders.

Garrett began to speak, snapping me out of meandering thoughts.

He introduced himself as Detective Chief Inspector Blackwood, and the women as Special Constable Sarah Lewis, the community liaison officer, and Mrs. Karyn Montpellier, Parish Councillor. The community liaison officer raised a hand and gave a girlish wave whilst behind Karyn's tight smile I sensed great tension.

Do they know he's a werewolf?

Stop it, Liv! You don't know that. You're just letting your imagination run away with you.

As I listened Garrett explain the reason for the meeting I watched him carefully, my mind transforming him into a muscular and towering wolfman. I sighed. Would I really mind if it were true? Was it really a problem if my boyfriend transmogrified into a howling beast once a month? It was a bit like my hormonal imbalances—they could throw me into a vile mood too.

Being a werewolf isn't exactly the same as being menopausal!

But I can be a beast!

Being hormonally challenged and a bit grouchy isn't the same, Liv! Werewolves hunt—people!

Well, we all eat meat.

I sighed. I loved Garrett with all my heart and that love was messing with my judgement. If Garrett was the Beast, then he was a killer. A killer who ripped his victims to shreds.

I sighed again and shook my head. It couldn't be true. The man standing before me, talking in earnest about how the police force were doing their very best to catch the killer, couldn't be one himself.

Teams had been scouring the moors, he informed us, and all avenues of enquiry were being followed. A woman close to me grunted. "Huh! If they were doing what they should be doing this would be over by now."

Her companion agreed. "What I want to know is why they've banned the television and newspapers. It should be on the national news but nothing, not even a story in the local paper. They've put a stop to it. Censorship! That's what that is."

The woman huffed. "It would have done wonders for business!"

Her companion nodded. "Would have brought in tourists."

"They could make a film of it. Imagine that, Sandra. If they make a film! There'll be actors and a film crew. It would be lucrative for the village. Your B&B would be full."

She nodded. "And your cafe would be packed."

Garrett's presentation had finished, and he asked the audience if they had any questions.

The disgruntled B&B owner stood up, raising her hand for attention.

He pointed at her.

"What I want to know is why you've banned the telly and papers from reporting on the murders? We need some proper reporting on it."

"Good for you, Kelly," her companion whispered.

Garrett cleared his throat. "This is a very sensitive point in our investigation. We've asked that the media don't report on it at present. We have a dangerous situation that if made public could impede our investigation."

"But people have a right to know! It's dangerous on them moors."

Again he coughed to clear his throat, obviously uncomfortable with the turn the questions were taking.

"My concern is that publicity will bring people to the village—so more people means more chance of someone being attacked."

"We could do with more people," she replied. "More people in the village is a good thing. Think of the business it could bring in."

There were a few murmurs of agreement and others of dissent.

"I understand your concerns, but safety is my priority at this moment."

"So tell people not to go on the moors!" a young woman shouted.

"Officers will be on patrol," Garrett assured.

"We all know who did it!" A man called from the back. The room turned to look. Supporting himself with a cane, was a man of at least seventy.

"That's Janet's husband," the B&B owner hissed to her companion. "One of the women the Beast killed all those years ago."

"I can assure you that we are not ruling out any avenues of investigation," Garrett said with non-committal diplomacy.

"It's Leonard Dimmock. They let him out of prison two weeks ago," the victim's husband shouted. "Tell me this Mr. Detective, why haven't you arrested him?"

Karyn Montpellier's lips pursed, and she nodded in agreement.

For a moment Garrett seemed confused and then turned slightly away from the audience to the community liaison officer.

"See! He doesn't know what's going on!" the woman in front of me said. "No wonder more women are being killed when the police don't even know what we know!"

Garrett's face drained of colour as the Special Constable continued to talk to him.

He cleared his throat. "You are correct Mr. Hastings, that Leonard Dimmock has been released from prison."

The room erupted. Karyn Montpellier's smile was triumphant.

"How can they let a killer out?"

"He's a murderer!"

"Oh, my God. The Beast is back!"

"You need to be warning people! If he's back, then none of us are safe!"

"It's like the Yorkshire Ripper—it'll be years before they catch him!"

"Please!" Garrett raised his hands and the room quieted. "Rest assured that we are doing everything we can to find the killer-"

"It's Dimmock! Go and arrest him."

"My team will follow up on that line of enquiry."

Karyn Montpellier stood, and the room quieted. "Please, everyone, we must remain calm. I can assure you that everything possible is being done to find the perpetrator of these crimes. The Beast, Leonard Dimmock, may be out of prison, but I can assure you that if he is in the area, we will find him and place him back where he belongs.

"Too right!"

"How can it be anyone else? He's doing exactly what he did before—killing people on the moors—even the method is the same. It's him."

"I share your concerns," Karyn placated.

"If he's out there, he'll kill again!"

The tension in the room was palpable and chatter rose. Karyn raised her hand and it quieted. I was impressed with the respect the gathered crowd had for her; she seemed able to control the level of noise in the room as though adjusting the volume on a radio.

"DCI Blackwood and his team will find the murderer," she stated. "I have every confidence in our local constabulary."

"He didn't even know that Dimmock was out of prison!" Mr. Hastings heckled. "How can he call himself a copper?" The man's tone was scathing.

"Too busy chasing speeding cars!"

"Or investigating tweets!"

Garrett remained calm despite the heckling although I noticed a flash of annoyance in his eyes.

Karyn turned to Mr. Hastings. "As you know, my father, PC Ernest Idle, was instrumental in catching the Beast of Wolfstane Moor and bringing him to justice. As his daughter, and in his memory, I can promise that, on his behalf, and on behalf of our very capable local police force, that we won't let you down."

Karyn returned to sitting.

The crowd settled and Garrett seemed relieved. "Thank you, Mrs. Montpellier." He turned his attention back to the crowd. "Are there any more questions?" A dozen people raised their hands.

I wanted to ask him outright if he was the Beast. Did he change at the full moon? Was the room at Blackwood Manor for him? Instead, as he began to answer questions, I slipped out of the hall and made my way back to the car, my nerves frayed.

Chapter Twelve

I sat in my car gathering myself before heading for the restaurant and by the time I arrived Garrett was already parked outside. He stepped out of his car to greet me as I pulled into the adjacent parking slot. My stomach churned and my heart began to thud. Being with Garrett always gave me that flutter of excitement, but now it was joined by an injection of fear. I took a breath to ease the tension and greeted him with a smile. He took my hand and placed a kiss on my cheek, caught my eyes then folded me in his arms.

"So good to see you," he said, his voice warm and sincere as he pressed me against his chest. It was muscular. He exuded strength. I revelled in his closeness.

My heart beat harder. This moment was everything to me. Everything I had hoped for. That Garrett wanted me felt like a miracle. I was fifty years old, a little on the heavy side, had daily battles with sprouting hairs on my upper lip, an ever-increasing stripe of white on my head, and chaotic hormones that caused me to overheat at the flick of a switch.

His embrace was comforting.

The Beast of Wolfstane Moor is a Blackwood.

His embrace was terrifying.

"It's good to see you too," I replied returning his embrace and enjoying the feeling of being held despite my growing unease. I inhaled his scent. It was fresh with an undertone of musk; delicious. Surely if he were a werewolf, I would smell it? There would be something primal wafting off of him surely?

"Shall we go inside?" he asked, taking my hand.

We entered the restaurant. It was unusually full, and, despite booking, we were asked to wait at the bar. Garrett ordered a low alcohol beer for himself, and I ordered a mocktail.

"I'm sorry that I couldn't pick you up," he said. "You could have had a proper drink then."

A proper drink would help me relax but I knew, from previous experience, that a proper drink would weaken my self-control. In my state, the clashing of my chaotic hormones with my unpredictable magick could lead to a scene. "It's fine, really." I sipped my mocktail. "This is delicious."

The minutes passed and we talked about our day. I showed him the bangle my aunts had given me. He seemed impressed. "You're definitely in the fold now then," he said as he held my hand to inspect the intricate designs. "One of the ..." He stopped, glanced around, and said in a low voice, "coven. Is that a fire dragon?" Holding my hand up, he peered at the creature. "It is. It's biting the hog's tail." He chuckled then ran a finger across the raised form of the creature but quickly pulled it away as though burned. "It bit me!"

I laughed. "What?"

"It stung! When I ran my finger over it, I felt it move and then it ... bit me."

"Don't be daft," I said looking down at the bangle. The creatures remained rigid with no evidence of movement.

"Look!" Garrett held out his hand. A pinprick of blood welled at the tip of his index finger. "I'm telling you, Liv. That thing just bit me."

"That's impossible," I replied, still holding onto the last vestiges of denial about my new reality.

"In our world, Liv, nothing is impossible." He raised a brow, then took a sip of his beer after dabbing the blood from his finger with a napkin. The spot bloomed on the tissue.

I studied the bangle with awe and a flash of dread.

They come alive when there is an existential threat to the coven.

As I took a sip of my mocktail, my hand trembled; adrenaline was beginning to flow, and I felt a familiar rising heat at my core.

They say that the Beast is a Blackwood.

"Your table is ready, madame, monsieur." The maitre'd ushered us to our table, his French accent as fake as his smile. He seemed on edge, did not make eye contact, and when he did glance at Garrett, it was with a flicker of unease.

I ordered pan-fried salmon and Garrett ordered a steak, the largest they had to offer, cooked rare.

Of course he would. If he's a werewolf, he's likely to want it raw!

Sitting opposite him as we waited for our meal to be delivered, he regaled me with amusing stories but, as I listened, I began to see him in a new light. He was a large man, over six foot tall, with broad shoulders and little fat. In fact he was muscular and in great shape for a man over fifty.

Well, he will be if he's a werewolf—they're always muscular in the films.

And then there was the dark beard and the dark hairs on his arms. Even his fingers had dark hairs. And then there were his teeth. The canines were particularly long, white, and perfectly shaped, but they protruded a little more than was usual below the other teeth.

All the better to eat you with, my dear!
Would his eyes glow beneath the full moon?
All the better to see you with!
"Liv!"
I was brought back to the conversation with a start.
He laughed. "You were away with the fairies."
I managed a laugh in return. "Don't! Given what I have to put up with at work that's not impossible!"
"They're growing on you though," he said with a grin, "your little helpers."
"More of a hindrance than a help sometimes, but yes, they're kind of growing on me. They don't freak me out as much as they used to." In the past they'd been as terrifying as flying mice, but I was getting used to them.
It was then that I noticed the scratch at his temple and several marks on his hands where scratches had scabbed over.
"You're hurt!" I blurted.
"What?"
"I mean ... there's a scratch on your head ... and on your hands."
He glanced down at his hands. "Oh, yes. I was in the garden. A briar attacked me." He offered me a wry grin.
The waitress arrived with our dinner. Blood oozed from Garrett's steak, and I watched as he placed a large chunk in his mouth, watched as sharp canines bite down into the flesh.
"Liv, are you alright?"
"What? Oh, yes. Sorry, just-"
"Away with the fairies? Again." He laughed then took a sip of his beer.

My heart pounded. I had to say something. "Something like that. I was just thinking about the murder on the moors. Mrs. Driscoll was quite graphic."

"Oh?"

"Yes, she said the victim had been shredded, her words, although she claims they're from an official source."

"Who?"

"One of the officers on the case. His wife is a friend of hers."

He nodded and cut into another chunk of bleeding steak. "It's true. The woman was in a terrible state, but you mustn't worry; we've recruited men from other forces to help with the investigation."

"People were suggesting that she had been attacked by an animal!" I watched his response with interest. He didn't seem surprised and only nodded. He placed another chunk of steak in his mouth, and I watched as a spot of blood sat on his lip and began to trickle down his chin. He quickly mopped it with a serviette.

"They say it's the Beast of Wolfstane Moor!" I blurted. "The real Beast and not Leonard Dimmock!"

Garrett stared at me for a moment then glanced around the room. "That's just a myth, Liv."

"It is?"

"Yes, an old legend."

"Well what killed the woman then? Could it have been a wild animal?"

"We don't have bears or tigers around here, Liv, and we've checked for any escaped animals from local zoos and wildlife parks. No wolves, bears, tigers, or lions are unaccounted for."

"Then could it be Leonard Dimmock? The man they released from prison? He killed those women when we were teenagers."

"It's an ongoing investigation so I really shouldn't say, and I couldn't mention it at the meeting, but ... we believe it's an escapee from Broadmoor. They've had several inmates go missing recently. One of them is of particular interest."

"But we're nowhere near Broadmoor!"

"True, but the criminally insane can use public transport as well as anyone. Or he could have walked. He's been on the run for a few weeks now."

The story was plausible, but I sensed that Garrett was lying.

He placed a hand over mine. "You mustn't worry. We're doing all we can to apprehend the perpetrator. He'll be back behind bars before you know it."

"I hope so," I said.

"Just don't go onto the moors," he warned.

"I won't," I promised.

More uneasy than ever, I excused myself and made a trip to the ladies to collect myself. The heat at my core was like rising panic only barely suppressed and I had a distinct tingle in my fingers. A spark hit the tap as I reached to turn it on.

Breathe, Livitha. Calm down.

Back at the table I continued to eat my salmon whilst Garrett continued to chew through his rare and bleeding steak.

When did Emily Blunt realise that Benicio Del Toro was the Wolfman? It ended badly for them. He died in the woods. Would Garrett die on the moors as the grimoire prophesied?

A spark hit my glass as I reached for it and bounced from its surface with a chink, landing as an ember on the tablecloth, turning black as it hit the white fabric.

Breathe!

"Liv, are you alright? You seem on edge tonight. Has the murder upset you that much?"

I could only nod as the heat at my core intensified. Sparks crackled as I hid my hands beneath the table.

"You mustn't worry. I would never let anything happen to you."

Unless you turn into a raging werewolf suffused with the instinct to kill.

Tomorrow was a full moon.

What made the scratches in the turret room, Garrett? "Really, I'm fine," I lied. "Just a long day. My aunts turned it into a training day. It was draining."

He nodded as though he understood.

I wanted to tell him about how I'd lost control of my powers and hit Old Mawde on the backside but then it would lead to Lucifer's sly comment, and he would know what I now suspected—that Garrett, the man I loved most in the world, could be the Beast of Wolfstane Moor! A maniacal killer!

I reached for my glass. Sparks flew. The glass knocked over, spilling what remained of my mocktail. Embers fizzed in the liquid and fell as black spots on the white cloth. Tendrils of smoke rose from the table.

"Sorry!" I whispered, frantically dabbing at a glowing ember eating its way through the cotton. The maitre'd glared at me from across the room.

Garrett sat, chunk of steak held on a raised fork, mouth agape, fangs ready to bite down on the bleeding meat. Lucifer, his black coat shining in the yellow light, sat beside the bar watching, his eyes trained on Garrett. He disappeared when I threw him a glare.

As dinner continued, the conversation was stilted, and I was relieved when Garrett's mobile rang, and our evening ended as he was called into work.

We parted with a kiss, but I drove home in a cloud of confusion. I was being ridiculous. Garrett wasn't the Beast of Wolfstane Moor. He couldn't be. Life was just not that cruel. Was it?

Chapter Thirteen

That night I dreamt of Garrett, but in those dreams, he morphed into the creature that had saved me from the imp that had slipped through from the other realm and had attacked me in the Black Woods. In my dream this incident melded with my discovery of the turreted room. I dreamt as though reliving it.

The heavy door swung open to reveal an uncarpeted room panelled in dark wood and dominated by a bed with four massive posts. Unlike a four-poster bed, the bedposts weren't topped by a curtain rail, nor were they intricately carved or pleasantly shaped. Instead, they resembled gateposts and stood at least six feet high. Heavy rings were bolted to them. To the side of the bed was a heavy and throne-like chair and I noticed with growing unease that the chair was fitted with shackles constructed of a padded leather band topped by a metal cuff. Once strapped in, it would be impossible to escape.

Scooping Lucifer into my arms, needing to feel the comfort of his being, I noticed the damaged panelling. The wainscotting had been scored in great arcs. In places it was splintered and in others gouged down to the bricks, damaged by an incredible and destructive force.

My guts gave a queasy flip. The place had an unnerving energy, not black, but dark. Rage and pain had festered there. My original thought had been that I'd walked into a chamber of torture! Now I suspected it was a cell of restraint—one to keep a cursed man chained whilst the lycanthrope within tried to take over!

Outside, an owl's hoot pierced the night.

I woke with a palpitating heart and sweat beading at my temples. My pyjama top was soaked and there was a sour smell to my sweat. I checked the bedside clock, it read three am, far too early to rise but I was wide awake and infused with a sense of doom so intense that for several moments I clutched the covers to my chin. After several minutes of falling in and out of sleep I managed to lose myself once again to unconsciousness. The dreams continued though, and I found myself in woodland, hiding behind the trees as the beast sought me.

As the grey light of morning filtered through my curtains, I was woken by the pounce of Lucifer jumping on my belly and then clawing at the duvet. Sharp talons pricked my thigh. A familiar was meant to be a witch's servant, a domestic help, and a companion in magick, but Lucifer was becoming overtly mean as well as demanding.

"If you want breakfast, you just have to ask," I complained. "Piercing my skin at six am, really is not necessary."

"It is totally necessary," he said and gave a final gouge at my thigh through the duvet before jumping back onto my chest, flicking his tail in my face then jumping to the floor. Thankfully, my eyes were firmly shut; Lucifer's rear was the last thing I wanted in my face at that time in the morning or at any time for that matter. "You were snoring. Loudly. If I had sat here demure and obedient then I would never have been able to make myself heard; it was like a steam engine rolling over old rails."

"Thanks!"

"It's true and I'm quite sure that it is your hormone levels that are causing the issue."

"Hormone levels?"

"Yes. Just as with your beard, you have the snoring ability of a man. I do believe that's what happens when levels of testosterone are too high."

"I am not turning into a man, and I do not snore that loudly."

"How would you know? You were asleep."

"I'd know."

"Do you have a sore throat by any chance?"

My throat did feel a little dry and uncomfortable.

"You do. I can tell. So there you are. You have snored and snorted throughout the night with such relish that now your throat is sore."

I groaned then sat up. "My hormone levels are perfectly normal for a woman of my age. And listen, you're supposed to give me support, not make me feel bad about myself."

He looked away.

"A witch's familiar-"

"I know what you're going to say, but I have grievances. I shall be taking them to the Council." He swished his tail and strolled to the door.

"What? What grievances? What exactly are you talking about?" I flung off the bedclothes and followed the feline to the door, but he trotted along the landing then disappeared down the stairs ignoring my calls. The anxiety that had gripped me during the night intensified. Whatever was Lucifer talking about? What grievances could he have against me? As far as I knew I had done nothing to cause offence. With the sense of foreboding grinding within me, thoughts of visiting Garrett's Uncle Tobias that afternoon mingling with the revelation that

Garrett may be hiding a deadly secret, I took a shower then dressed for the day.

For a change, I was early and, after a quick breakfast, too perturbed by Lucifer's accusation to enter into anything but the lightest of conversation with my aunts, I left for the shop with nearly an hour to spare.

I decided to take a detour across the moors. It was foolish, but it was a need I could not ignore.

Driving to the higher ground, the woodlands giving way to undulating hills barren but for short grasses, moss and heathers, the logical part of me told me to turn around, but I had to know about the beast and the draw to investigate was irresistible.

I had done a little digging around and discovered the spot where the woman the beast had attacked had parked her car and I drove to the same spot. The moors were bleak and across the hills dark clouds cast black shadows across the land; despite my fleece, woollen hat, and gloves, the wind was biting.

As soon as I'd stepped out of the car, I sensed it, a dark energy, the remnants of the woman's final moments, her fear, her terror, her ... screams. I shuddered. The gypsy had told me to stay off the moors. Garrett had told me to stay off the moors. I knew that I should go back to the car, but something more than mere curiosity drew me onwards. Time passed and I lost sight of my car and climbed down a rocky outcrop to a gorge. Ahead white tape fluttered in the wind, trapped among the heather. Closer inspection revealed it to be the remnants of tape from the crime scene. 'POLICE LINE DO NOT CROSS' was printed across it in large blue letters. I was close but I didn't need the tape to tell me that. I could feel it, just as I felt it when

I had discovered Alice Yikkar, the Pendlewick crone who had met her death in Haligern Woods.

I followed my senses, the dark energy like a beacon, guiding me closer. I knew that the body had been removed, but I had expected more evidence of police involvement or surveillance. Where were the vehicles? Where was the team doing a finger-tip search of the area? Had they already searched and decided that no further action was to be taken? But Garrett had told me that they were doing everything they could to catch the per-petrator. Had he told me not to come onto the moors because then I'd see that nothing was being done? Had he called off the investigation for fear of being found out to be the murder-er himself? A wave of guilt washed over me. How could I sus-pect him? My love for Garrett was intense and only growing stronger. But what if he were the beast? What if he had killed the woman? Would I inform the police of what I knew?

Snitches wear stitches!

Or would I bury the knowledge deep in my psyche and ac-cept that side of him? Would I become the wife of the Wolf-man! Wife? Yes, that is exactly what I wanted to become to Garrett, but if he were cursed ...? My thoughts in turmoil, I continued down the ravine and came to a hard stop. It was here. This was the place where the woman had died. There was ev-idence too; small scraps of fabric caught in the heather, earth scuffed, the loam rich and dark against the moss. And then there was blood—brown, dark red in places where it lay thick. My mind's eye saw the attack, how the creature had surprised her from behind, how she had fought against it. It had been over quickly—at least that's what I told myself—it eased the horror.

The place would carry her energy now and I wondered if it was possible to cleanse a space outdoors as you could a house.

The wind bit at my cheeks and I moved further down the ravine to where a narrow stream flowed crystal clear over dark rocks. I followed it to the point where it disappeared back into the earth and then climbed up the now steep banks to higher ground. A solitary tree grew from behind a large boulder. At the top, the vista opened up and a large hill rose from the undulating land. Halfway up its side sat a single storey cottage with outbuildings forming a courtyard.

A wisp of smoke spiralled from the chimney.

Chapter Fourteen

"I had no idea anyone lived out here," I muttered and began to tramp towards the house. Despite the thin trail of smoke that curled from the chimney there were no lights shining from the windows and I guessed that whoever lived there had left for the day. I walked for several minutes then stopped abruptly. In the distance, moving along the winding moor road, and heading towards the house, was a car. I bobbed down, wishing that I hadn't worn my bright pink fleece. I would be obvious at a distance and, apart from the ravine I'd just left, there was little to hide behind other than the odd cluster of heather.

The car moved closer then drew up to the house. A man got out. I recognised him immediately—Garrett!

As he closed the door a man stepped out from the house. As they met, they embraced, spoke for several moments, then turned their attention to my direction. I shuffled back, heartbeat hammering like a tympany drum, flattening myself against the ground, hoping that the low hillock was enough to hide me. The grimoire's prophecy repeated in my mind.

'Upon the moor his heart will beat.

Upon the hearth his blood will seep.

The Beast will fall, and you will weep.

The Blackwood Curse is yours to keep.'

Raising my head, relieved that the men's attention turned away from me, I decided to retrace my steps and return to my car. There was no way I could get close to the house without being seen and Garrett had warned me not to go out onto the moors; he would be annoyed, or worse, disappointed in me.

I shuffled backwards to a point where the ground lowered then ran in an awkward crouched style back towards the ravine until I was sure that Garrett and whoever he was with at the cottage wouldn't be able to see me.

What was he doing there? Most likely following up on his investigations. So he hadn't abandoned it. I was just ignorant of the process. He was interviewing the man no doubt to ask him what he'd seen that day. What he'd heard. But why had he embraced him? The foolishness of my efforts washed over me, and I was thankful that I had been far enough away not to be recognised. Unless ... unless Garrett had seen my car! Several panicked seconds followed until I realised that there were other routes to the cottage and that he'd probably taken one of them. I checked my phone; if he had seen my car, he would have tried to contact me. There were no messages. Relieved but feeling foolish, I made my way back through the ravine.

It was as I got to the top, with my car in sight, that I heard it.

Shattering the peaceful air of the moors, a howl erupted.

A howl. In the middle of the morning. On a moor where a woman had been mauled to death. More than mauled, 'shredded' according to Mrs. Driscoll.

I turned in the direction of the noise.

And stood paralysed.

In the far distance, but bounding in my direction, was a creature I recognised immediately although my mind refused to admit it.

A werewolf!

It took huge and powerful strides towards me.

What big fangs you have!

I gasped, turned back towards my car, and ran.

All the better to eat you with, my dear.

My car was close, closer than I was to the beast, but it was fast—really fast!

Heart pounding, breath coming hard, I powered forward, oblivious of the bitter wind and the rain that was starting to fall.

The next minutes were a blur, a desperate rush over uneven land. I stumbled twice, only just managing to keep my balance. I looked only forward, keys in hand, ready to unlock the door with a click. The last stretch of land rose up before me. I grasped the heather, propelled myself upwards, and reached the roadside. Breath coming hard, the pain in my chest intense, I clicked the door to unlocked, peering over the roof to the moor.

It was there.

Watching.

A yelp caught in my throat, and I swung the car door open and threw myself in. With trembling hands I started the engine aware of the approaching figure. I thrust the gears into first and, with a squeal of tyres, sped away, flooring the accelerator, and propelling the car ever faster, engine straining. Thankfully, the stretch of road was straight, and as I reached sixty miles an hour, I dared to check my rear-view mirror. The beast was nowhere to be seen but I didn't slow, instead I raced through the moors, checking my mirrors repeatedly, and only slowed once I reached the village boundary.

The beast was real. I had seen him. My stomach lurched. Garrett! He had gone into the house! I hadn't seen him leave. What if he had been attacked?

Pulling over to the side of the road, I fumbled in my bag for my phone and, with trembling hands, dialled his number. The phone rang, then rang again, then went to voicemail.

Startled by a knock at my car window, I dropped the phone and stared into the dark eyes of the gypsy-witch. I gasped with momentary relief.

She rapped again and I rolled the window down, still shaking, heart pounding.

"What you want, lady?"

"Nothing!" I blurted.

Her eyes narrowed and she reached inside the car and grabbed my hand. A smile curled at the side of her mouth. "Hah! You did not listen. I told you not to go onto the moor but what are my efforts worth, huh? Nothing. I cannot change your fate. Now he knows as I knew he would."

"I have no idea what you're talking about," I lied.

"Of course not," she said with a smirk. "You know nothing. All is dark when you search, but you will know. Soon it will be clear."

"Tell me! Tell me what I have to do."

"The Beast will be yours to keep."

I gasped. "How do you know that?"

"You know how I know, witch! We are the same you and I. You know. I know."

"But what does it mean?"

"I can help you, but it will take you to the dark side of magick." The woman's eyes locked to mine. "Come with me and I will show you all the magick that you need."

"I'm not sure ... Isn't it dangerous?"

"Hah! There is danger, sure, but there is great power too. Come!" she beckoned. "Come with me."

I was about to open the door and follow her when Garrett's car drew up beside mine. The passenger side window rolled down. "Are you alright?" he leant across the seat.

I nodded. "Yes," I replied, awash with guilt.

"Is this woman causing you trouble?"

"Pah!"

"No! I ... I stopped to answer the phone," I lied.

The woman raised a finger to her lips, her back to Garrett. "Come to me later. There is much I can teach you." Ignoring Garrett, she turned and walked back into the mist.

"How do you know her?" he asked.

"I don't know her. She's a gypsy, I think."

He held my gaze then nodded. "Are we still on for this afternoon?" he asked.

With emotions whirling and on the verge of tears as relief and guilt flooded me, I could only nod.

"Are you on the way to the shop?"

Again, I nodded.

"Shall I pick you up from there?" he asked now with a slight frown.

"Yes!" I blurted. "Yes, that will be fine."

"You sure you're okay?"

"Oh, yes!"

"Good. Well, I'll see you later then."

"Yes! See you."

His frown deepened. The window rolled back up and he pulled away. I breathed a sigh of relief and sat for several minutes forcing myself to become calm before continuing on to the shop. With the fear that Garrett had been harmed no longer a concern and my brush with the gypsy-witch's temptation behind me, my thoughts returned to the house on the moors. Who lived there? I had to know.

Chapter Fifteen

Garrett picked me up as promised and though my fingers fizzed and several sparks hit the dashboard as we drove to Blackwood Manor, his easy manner and amusing conversation helped me to relax. However, the journey there was a torment as I remembered the gypsy-witch's prophecy and my suspicions about Garrett. Add to that the werewolf that had chased me off the moors and I was on the verge of becoming hysterical. I forced myself to remain calm and focused on Garrett's conversation before I became a jabbering wreck and embarrassed myself once again in front of his Uncle Tobias.

We rolled up outside the manor house to an overcast sky and mist beginning to form. The air was damp and the spaces between the trees that circled the house dark. Miles from the village, surrounded by forest, Blackwood Manor was the perfect place to hide from society if the lycanthropic gene ran through your family's line.

I flinched as Garrett slipped his arm across my shoulder. He tensed. I grabbed his hand. He sensed my unease, and it was causing tension between us, the last thing I wanted. The revelations of the past two days had been difficult to process, and I was still reeling from this morning, but I had to get through afternoon tea without causing a scene or spoiling it by being on edge. I determined in that moment to shelve my fear, and my concerns, and meet Uncle Tobias with a smile and easy, friendly energy. I loved Garrett and whatever the truth was about the room in the turret we would get through it—as long as he didn't eat me first of course!

As we reached the wide stone steps that led up to the heavy doors and the entrance hallway to Blackwood Manor, Garrett turned to me. "I know that you're nervous-"

"Is it that obvious?" I tried a laugh, but it stuck in my throat, and I only managed a noise like a strangled cat.

Garrett snorted and raised his brows then stroked my cheek. "Listen, don't worry. Uncle Tobias—well, he's a little eccentric, but a good man really. I know you two have had your issues, but he's looking forward to this afternoon; he knows how important you are to me."

I swallowed, emotion rising, and my vision blurred. *Don't cry, Liv!* "I hope he doesn't hold it against me?"

"What?"

"Hitting him with Arthur! I could have killed him."

"Is that what all this is about?" Arms embraced me and I was crushed to his chest. Firm muscle, softened only a little by middle age, pressed against my cheek. My nose was forced into his armpit, and I quickly began to run out of oxygen as he hugged me and continued to talk, placating me with soothing words. He was strong. I tried to move back but, caught in his embrace, I was stuck. "There really is no need to worry."

I thumped his back then gasped as he released me, sucking in air.

"You okay?"

I nodded. "Just need fresh air," I managed.

He looked taken aback then glanced at his armpit. "I showered."

"No! Not that. You smell great. I couldn't breathe."

"Oh! Sorry. Sometimes I don't know my own strength."

A shock of pink lipstick was smeared across his shirt.

He reached into his pocket and pulled out a tissue. "Here, your lipstick." He pointed to his lips then offered me the tissue.

"Is it a mess?"

"Not too bad, just kind of smeared over your lip."

The lipstick wasn't meant to come off. I'd used it once before and it had stained my lips for days and worn it today as I didn't want lipstick to stain Uncle Tobias' teacups. I wiped at my top lip. "Is it okay now?"

Garrett gave my lips a brief glance, nodded, then took my hand. "Come on."

Uncle Tobias was waiting in the drawing room as we entered. A fire had been lit and was filling the room with warmth and a pleasant glow.

"Uncle, here's Livitha to see you."

"Ah, yes! I've been waiting."

I took a step forward and he flinched taking a backwards step, hands raised as though fending me off. I stalled, mortified.

"Uncle!"

His shocked expression broke into a smile, and he began to chuckle. "Forgive me, Livitha. I couldn't resist."

"Oh," I managed then joined in the laughter.

"That was unfair," Garrett chided in a friendly manner.

"Oh, I know, but it does get boring around here. I haven't had much fun since Livitha's notorious visit. I was rather hoping for some excitement to be honest."

"There's always plenty of that with Livitha about, Uncle, believe me." He threw me a knowing smile. "Trouble does seem to follow her."

Uncle Tobias chuckled. "Well, we could do with a bit of livening up around here. I hope she doesn't disappoint." He raised his brows and smiled.

Garrett laughed and slipped an arm around my waist. "Oh, she never disappoints."

Relief flooded me. Uncle Tobias had obviously forgiven me for nearly killing him. We chatted and joked, and Uncle Tobias promised to show me around the house after we'd eaten our tea and biscuits. "But only the lower rooms," he said. "The place is far too large and rambling to show you the others but, I'm sure, in the future, you'll have plenty of time to explore the house yourself." He glanced at Garrett who quickly looked away. There was some unspoken comment between them, and I felt an inkling of unease creeping back; I had already seen the upstairs rooms when I'd searched the house for Arthur, Aunt Loveday's grimoire, and found it clutched in Uncle Tobias's arms as he slept. I felt the flush of guilt begin to spread at the base of my throat.

Garrett cleared his throat and was about to speak when the bell at the front door rang.

"Who the devil can that be? Are you expecting more guests, my boy?"

"No, uncle."

"Then it must be a delivery, but it's awfully late. The shop normally delivers in the morning." He glanced outside the window, and I noticed a quick look into the sky. "I don't like it when they come this close to twilight. Makes me nervous." He sighed then turned to me. "We're out here on our own, Livitha. Your aunts must feel it too. Of course, I have Hector to help guard the place and Patrick, of course."

Voices filled the hallway and then came a rap at the door. It swung open to reveal Patrick, Uncle Tobias' doorman-cum-butler.

"Whatever is it, Patrick. Who comes here at this time of night?"

"It's a lady, sir."

"A lady."

"Yes. She's waiting in the lobby."

"And ... what does she want?"

"She wants to see you, sir."

He grumbled. "Excuse me, Livitha. I shall leave you in Garrett's capable hands whilst I speak to our visitor."

Uncle Tobias left the room closing the door behind him. Garrett peered out of the window. I followed but only the edge of the driveway could be seen from this angle and what we could see was empty of any vehicles.

"Who is it?" I asked.

"If I could see through walls I'd tell you," Garrett laughed though he seemed on edge. Perhaps, like me, he was feeling the strain of the afternoon although it seemed to be going well.

Minutes later, Uncle Tobias re-entered the room. The jovial smile and ruddy cheeks had been replaced by a dazed look. His skin had lost all colour.

"Whatever is the matter, Uncle?"

He beckoned Garrett to him. "You had better come and see. I'm at a loss for words."

Something was wrong. Very wrong. It could only mean that there had been terrible news. Perhaps someone close to them had died.

I followed Garrett out of the room and into the entrance hall. A young woman stood in the centre. She was pretty with large green eyes framed by dark lashes. The blonde hair that fell down to her waist looked natural. She held her arms beneath her belly, her heavily pregnant belly. Her eyes lit up when she saw Garrett.

He was silent as she stepped forward.

"You can go now, Patrick," Uncle Tobias instructed the butler.

Unease grew to a stone-like lump in my stomach. I felt on the precipice of some terrible revelation.

"I'm terribly sorry, Livitha," Uncle Tobias said as he walked past me to the drawing room.

Sorry?

"Garrett!" the woman gushed and walked over to him. "I'm sorry, but I had to find you."

He simply nodded.

"I know that we said we shouldn't, but I had to tell you about the baby."

Again he nodded.

I tugged at his sleeve. "What's going on?" The stone in my belly grew heavier.

The girl caught my gesture and frowned. "I'm having his baby."

The stone in my belly exploded. "No!"

"Yes!" she countered. "Yes, I am."

Chapter Sixteen

I don't recall what happened next. I don't remember getting home.

Aunt Beatrice knocked on my door as I lay like a forlorn teenager, head buried in a now wet and snotty pillow. "Livitha!"

I grunted a response.

"I've brought you a cup of tea. Aunt Euphemia told me that you came home in a ... well, upset."

My head remained buried in the pillow.

"I've brought you a bowl of apple crumble. We didn't have custard made, so I've poured on some cream."

I tapped the bedside table. "Put it there." Another sob erupted.

I felt the bed press down next to me as the slight figure of my aunt eased herself to sit.

"She's been like this for hours! Just preposterous!"

"Shoo!"

"Well-."

"Shoo, Lucifer before I hex you."

"How very dare you!"

"Go on now. Betsy is waiting for you in the kitchen. She's feeling rather neglected of late."

"Well, I have my reas-"

"Tell me about them later, Lucifer. I need to speak to Livitha. Close the door on your way out."

I heard the vexatious feline sniff in disapproval then pad to the door. It closed with a thud and then Aunt Beatrice laid a hand on my shoulder. Another sob erupted; her kindness making my efforts at holding in my emotions crumble.

"Whatever is the matter, Livitha. I know it's something terrible but-"

"Garrett's having a baby!" I wailed. The words were muffled, barely audible, unclear.

"What, dear? I didn't catch that."

I sat up.

"Oh my goodness! You are in a sorry state." Aunt Beatrice thrust a tissue at me then followed it with the bowl of crumble.

I accepted it and took a spoonful, swallowing quickly, my nose blocked.

"Now, take a sip of tea."

I took a sip of tea. A warm sensation started at the back of my throat then spread throughout my body. My muscles relaxed, the throbbing in my head softened, and the pain in my heart dulled. The tea was laced with elixir. I took another sip and then a gulp.

Several minutes passed. Aunt Beatrice waited patiently.

"This is worse than Pascal," I said, self-pity welling once more.

"What is worse than Pascal?"

"Garrett!" I managed.

"Has Garrett ... betrayed you?"

I nodded then sniffed.

"Why the mendacious toad! The philandering, adulterous, conniving toad!"

"We aren't married."

"Nor shall you ever be."

"He hadn't even asked me."

"Nor shall he ever!"

I took another spoonful of crumble and sat back against the headboard, wallowing in the fuzzy warmth the elixir had spread throughout my body. My breathing eased. I no longer wanted to cry.

"Tell me exactly what has happened. The Haligern Coven will not stand for one of our sisters being deceived or rejected or thrown on the scrap heap!"

"You're not helping!"

"It cannot go unchallenged, Livitha. This is coven business."

"He's *my* boyfriend." I sniffed. "Was my boyfriend—the only man I ever truly loved." I fell into a fresh bout of sobbing.

"Oh, dear!"

The bedroom door opened, and Aunt Euphemia stepped in. "Has she told you, Beatrice? Why Livitha, whatever it is, I'm sure that we can help."

"Garrett is having a baby!" I wailed.

The room grew silent.

"A baby?"

I nodded. "Yes! And with a beautiful woman. She's young and lovely and doesn't have hair on her chin."

In the corner Lucifer snorted.

"Go away, Lucifer!"

"Pah!"

"But how?"

I shrugged.

"When is the baby due?"

"By the look of her belly, any day."

"Ah."

"What 'Ah'?"

"Well, then take heart, dear. It must have happened in the past."

"Of course it happened in the past," said Aunt Euphemia.

"What I mean is that it must have occurred before Blackwood and Livitha began seeing one another."

"Ah, I see. So he hasn't betrayed her."

"No. He has been foolish for certain, but a deceiver perhaps not."

"That must be ascertained."

"Indeed."

I listened as they discussed my relationship with Garrett between themselves, scooping mouthfuls of the large bowlful of crumble until it was scraped clean then finished the tea. The warmth of the tea and crumble was comforting, and I leant back, eyes puffy from crying, and closed my eyes.

"This has been the worst day of my life," I stated.

"Surely not."

"It has. It has been the day from hell."

"More elixir, Euphemia, please."

Aunt Euphemia disappeared then reappeared minutes later with a pot of tea and the bottle of elixir.

Minutes passed. I knew that I should be honest and explain about my encounter with the gypsy-witch and the beast on the moor this morning, but something held me back.

"Now," said Aunt Beatrice. "I feel quite sure that this can all be sorted out. If the woman is pregnant with his baby ... well ..."

I waited for her to resume but she remained silent. It struck me then that Garrett hadn't tried to call me or even send a text. I was back right where I had been when I discovered Pascal's infidelity with our neighbour—alone, lonely, and on the shelf. Thrown away like a pair of old knickers! Like Selma, the woman was younger and more attractive than me. She also had a huge advantage over me—she was fertile. Not menopausal. And she was carrying his baby. As far as I knew, his first child.

"It's over," I said. "Just over."

"Perhaps it's for the best, dear."

My heart sank within me. She was right. Garrett was going to be a father; he could have his happy little family. I wouldn't stand in his way. My head throbbed and as the elixir took hold, I sank into a deep sleep untroubled by dreams.

I woke to the moon's light shining through the gap in my bedroom curtains. Eyelids still puffy with crying, senses overwhelmed by Garrett's impending fatherhood, I stumbled out of bed. One thought overrode all others; I had to discover who lived at the house on the moors.

My aunts had long since gone to bed and the downstairs rooms sat in darkness. In the kitchen, glowing embers gave the room warmth and moonlight fell on the table but cast dark shadows. Grabbing my keys from the hook behind the door and my coat from the peg in the hallway, I made my way to the front door.

"Where do you think you're going at this time of night, Mistress Erickson?"

"Lucifer! You startled me."

"Well? Where?"

"Out."

"Out? It is the middle of the night. Ladies do not go out in the middle of the night, at least not ones of good repute. Are you a woman of ill-repute, Livitha?"

"I am not, and you know it!" I snapped.

"Well, I for one, and I will not be alone, cannot for the life of me imagine an innocent reason for you to leave the house alone in the middle of the night."

Irked at his attitude, I told him the truth. "I'm going up onto the moors. There's a house there. I have to know who lives there."

"It's empty. It has been for years."

"Well, there's someone living there now."

"And why is that your business? Pray, tell, do."

"Well ... it's not my business, but ... well, it doesn't matter. I'm going there to find out."

"You do know that the Beast of Wolfstane Moor has returned, do you not?"

I paused. I did. I had seen it. I meant to confront it and make sure it was dealt with. "I can handle the beast. I've done it before." Plus, there was the offer of help from the gypsy-witch.

"Done it before? Do you mean that galumphing gargoyle in the Black Woods?"

"Yes. I dealt with it even without the knowledge I have now. I can deal with the Beast."

"Without resorting to dark magick?"

For several seconds Lucifer and I stared at one another. "Of course," I retorted. I hated lying but something inside was driving me on. I had to deal with the beast before it dealt with me, and if I had to take advice from the gypsy-witch, then so be it.

Lucifer strolled to the front door then turned to me. "I cannot allow you to pass."

"You cannot make me stay." Scooping the acerbic cat up, I placed it behind me in the hall.

"It is a mistake to leave, Livitha."

"Don't worry about me, I shall be back before breakfast."

I closed the door as he continued to stare and made my way to the car.

With the car door closed, I placed the key into the ignition then jumped as knuckles rapped at the window and a face loomed in at me. The door opened and Aunt Thomasin stared in. With her hair tucked up in her nightcap and her quilted dressing gown zipped up to her chin, she looked stern. "Whatever are you doing, Livitha Erickson?"

I knew I was in trouble. Behind her my other aunts had gathered. Dressed in their nightwear, they shivered in the cold.

"Come along inside! It is far too late to be going out."

"And cold!"

"Tell her to come in!"

"I have."

"Now, Livitha. It really isn't the done thing to go out into the middle of the night. Whatever would Uncle Raif say if he knew?"

"I'm not doing anything wrong! And anyway, I'm a grown woman."

"Yes, and one about to do something foolish."

I knew it was a bad idea, but in my emotional state my judgement wasn't rational.

"Let us sort this out, Livitha."

"No. This is my problem," I tried.

"The Beast of Wolfstane Moor is not your problem, dear."

I began to pull the door closed. If they continued to harangue me, I would eventually change my mind and I was determined to get to the bottom of the mystery. Who was in the farmhouse? And who was the Beast of Wolfstane Moor?

Held by my aunt, the door refused to close.

"I think we must intervene, sisters."

I turned the key and the engine growled into life.

"I do agree. It is the only way."

As I pushed the clutch down and changed the gear into first my foot slipped off the pedal and then my hands, suddenly stiff, slipped off the gear stick. The car stalled.

I screamed.

My hands had become hooves and my belly, now pushed up against the steering wheel was covered in black hair. And ... I had udders!

What have you done to me! "Ma-a-a-a! Ma-a-a-a!"

"Now, now, dear. Don't fret. This is for your own benefit."

"It's the only way. We have to be cruel to be kind."

"Indeed, Loveday."

I stared at my aunts, their faces now distorted, then flipped and landed with a twisting thump on the gravel before jumping to all fours. I headed towards the gateway but as I cantered across the driveway, I was yanked back by a rope thrown over my neck. Lassoed, I bleated, front legs hanging in the air.

"She's going to be feisty!"

"A night with Old Mawde will calm her."

Help! "Ma-a-a-a!"

"She does make a very handsome goat though!"

I lowered my head and took aim. "Ma-a-a-a!"

Chapter Seventeen

This cannot be happening!

The phrase repeated in my mind as I was pulled towards the goat pen. Ahead Old Mawde and Hegelina Fekkit were staring at the drama with great interest.

"This is not happening!" I shouted. In my head the words were clear, but they erupted from my throat as an angry bleat.

"It's for your own good," Aunt Thomasin said as she pulled me through the gate and into the field where the pen and its goats were kept. "We couldn't let you go up onto those moors—it's far too dangerous."

Lucifer! He told them. He had ratted on me. What happened to honour among familiars? What about loyalty?

Neck stretched forward as I dug my hooves into the ground and Aunts Euphemia and Thomasin pulled, I gave another angry bleat. I was not going to share a pen with those two old and cantankerous goats. I had watched them on numerous occasions, had to dodge their kicks when I'd milked them ... milked them! No way! I was not going to be milked. I yanked at the rope, pulling it out of my aunts' hands and broke free. I made a beeline for the gate, cantering at breakneck speed and hurtled forward. I would not be milked. This was just too much to bear.

"Get her, Beatrice!"

At the gate Aunt Beatrice stood spreadeagled. I lowered my head, panic overwhelming me. The phrases repeating, 'I will not be milked!'

"She's going to hit you, Beatrice! Be careful!"

Aunt Beatrice cackled, extended her arms, and threw out a shot of magical energy. The effect was instant, and I staggered, hit by the current, electrocuted by magick! I stumbled and then my legs buckled, and I sat, legs beneath me, too stunned to move. It wasn't painful but it was paralysing.

"Good shot!"

"Thank you. I have been practicing. They have a range at the Academy you know."

"A shooting range?"

"Yes, it's fully insulated so no chance of accidents." Standing beside me, she chuckled. "Well, you have surprised us, Livitha. Such spirit!"

"It's rather wonderful. I had been concerned that her experience with Pascal had done irreparable harm, but she is increasingly feisty, and her confidence grows."

"Hmm. We had better get this mess with Blackwood sorted out. Something about it stinks."

"Indeed, it does."

"And I had such high hopes. I even imagined that the family could be rehabilitated."

"Indeed."

"I'm still here!" I shouted, my angry bleat filling the air.

"She is cross! I think I'm rather glad I can't understand what she's saying."

"It has the tone of expletives."

"She can swear like a navvy when she puts her mind to it!"

"Tsk! Let's hope that she learns to channel this energy and make it useful. Put more effort into her studies—spells are rarely instinctive although she is lucky—the ancient ones have favoured her."

"Hmm."

They continued to talk about me, being far more candid about their opinions and thoughts than they ever would be if I were stood in front of them in my true form.

"Come along, Livitha. Old Mawde and Hegelina Fekkit are keen to meet you."

Aunt Thomasin snorted then Aunt Beatrice cackled.

I groaned, irked at being the object of their laughter, and glanced across the field. Now bathed in moonlight, both goats had left their pen and were staring our way.

"How long will this last?" I bleated.

"What is she saying, Beatrice? Can you still read her mind?"

"To an extent. She's complaining and wants to know how long the curse will last."

"Oh, it's not a curse. Just a transformation spell and the answer is as long as Loveday believes she's a danger to herself."

"This incident with Blackwood has skewed her thinking. She thinks she can take on the Beast of Wolfstane Moor."

"Impossible!"

"But not for us."

"I don't know ..."

"Loveday will know what to do. Livitha is a loose cannon and until we can get to the bottom of the issue, she will just have to remain with Old Mawde."

"No!" My bleat was plaintive.

"Poor thing. I hope that she will forgive us."

"Oh, I'm sure she will."

"I will not!" I bleated.

"Come along," Aunt Thomasin repeated, and pulled at the rope around my neck.

I rose on four unsteady legs. Aunt Thomasin led me towards the pen, earth squeezing between my cloven hooves, my udder swinging like a pendulum.

Horrified but defeated, a dejected prisoner being introduced to the other inmates for the first time, I headed for the darkest corner of the pen, avoiding Old Mawde's eyes.

"How the mighty do fall," she bleated as I passed her. Hegelina Fekkit joined her in a fit of cackling with a definitely nasty edge.

Both goats followed me into the pen then stood silent until my aunts had walked to the other side of the field and closed the gate.

"Well, well, well," said Hegelina Fekkit. "Look who we have here."

I had seen innumerable films where a new inmate was introduced to the 'population' and knew what was coming. I would have to prove myself stronger than them and, in my present form, my magical abilities muted, it would mean a physical fight. The day had started and ended badly but if the next hours, or Thor forbid, days, were to be endured, I would have to prove myself dominant. I turned to face them, hid my fear, and stared from one to the other.

"You can sleep outside," Old Mawde said.

"Yes, she can," agreed Hegelina. "This is our pen."

"No," I replied.

"Yes," Old Mawde insisted.

"Make me."

Without waiting for them to make the first move, I launched myself at Hegelina Fekkit. I'd observed that she was the most bullying and dominated Old Mawde, taking the best dandelions for herself and pushing her out of the way when she wanted a drink of water. Head down, I charged and caught her a glancing blow to the top of her front leg. She made a squealing bleat but quickly regained her balance and lowered her head against me. Over the next minutes I was head butted, thrown against the pen wall, and kicked but I did not back down and returned headbutt for headbutt, kick for kick. I had the added advantage—rage. Something inside me had clicked when the woman had claimed to be carrying Garrett's baby. I was devastated but more than that I was angry. Angry with the world. Angry with myself. Angry with the gods. Angry with Garrett for making such a fool of me. Angry with the fate the witch had said was mine. I would not die a rejected old fool at the hands of a werewolf. I was determined to get even, at whatever cost—even if that meant using the dark magick the gypsy-witch had promised.

With a final and decisive headbutt that caught Hegelina Fekkit at the side of her head I was victorious. She staggered then dropped to sit on her rump and made a feeble bleat.

I turned to Old Mawde. "You want some?"

Old Mawde took a step backwards and shook her head.

"So who is going to sleep outside now then?"

She avoided eye contact and didn't reply. I knew I had to press home my victory. "I'm sleeping inside. You and your friend will sleep outside." I took an aggressive step towards her. She bleated, turned, and trotted away to the far side of the field. Hegelina Fekkit followed.

"And stay there," I shouted as they galloped across the field. "Good riddance," I said and returned to the corner of the pen before lowering myself to the ground.

The victory was hollow and the night long but as dawn broke and grey light seeped into the pen, I finally managed to fall asleep. I dreamed of Garrett, his arm around the woman, she cradling their baby. I dreamed of the beast chasing me across the moors, snarling, its fangs revealed as it grew close, its face morphing into Garrett's. And then I was at the cottage looking inside where a fire glowed in the hearth and Garrett stood with his lover in an embrace, her huge belly between them. But the worst dream I had that night took me back to the moors where the woman laboured alone as the beast prowled. I held the new-born in my arms, cooing at its beauty until it opened yellow eyes and snapped at me with long and sharp fangs.

Deep sleep finally took me, and I woke to a cold morning, my breath billowing white, and the long snouts of Hegelina Fekkit and Old Mawde poking through the unglazed window as they watched.

I groaned as I remembered where and what I was.

Chapter Eighteen

The morning passed slowly. There was little to do in the field but munch on the grass or sleep. Too wound up in my own misery I didn't notice the absence of my aunts until Old Mawde strolled by, kicked at the door, then began to complain bitterly about the cruelty of neglect. "Those crones should be reported for abuse," she spat. "Leaving me to suffer like this. It's inhumane."

Hegelina Fekkit, who did not produce milk (my aunts had decided that given her temperament it was most likely that the milk would taste sour) cackled with vindictive delight. "We should report them to the RSPCA."

"Never heard of it."

"Royal Society for the Prevention of Cruelty to Animals."

"I'm not an animal!"

Hegelina scoffed. "What are you then?"

"She's a goat that identifies as a crone," I said with a bitter tone.

Both goats looked at me. "She's talking nonsense again."

"What does she mean?"

"I have no idea. Ignore her."

"I wish she would go away."

"So do I."

My presence seemed to have made the pair allies; I, the enemy.

Old Mawde groaned with discomfort, her udder full but, despite their unpleasantness, I wasn't spiteful enough to enjoy her pain. "I'm sure they'll be here soon," I placated. It was then that it dawned on me that it was unusually late. The sun was almost at its highest point, way past milking time. As I scanned the house for evidence of movement, Uncle Raif stepped out of the kitchen door and made his way to the garage. Too far away to make myself heard, a pointless effort given that he would only hear me bleat, I watched as he manoeuvred the car out of the garage and then drove away. There was no sign of my aunts. Time passed and Old Mawde continued to complain, and I grew increasingly concerned. My aunts never let Old Mawde go this long without being milked; they knew how much discomfort she would be in and although they were the ones who had kept her in this cursed state for centuries, they were not vindictive enough to cause her pain—at least not physical.

With the gate locked, trapping me in the field, I walked along the fence to a point where I could see the back of the house. The curtains were closed which was another oddity; my aunts religiously opened the curtains as soon as it was light. Something was wrong. I paced beside the fence, then placed my hooves on top of the gate to gain a better view. A car pulled into the drive.

Garrett!

Landing back on the grass with a thump I became agitated, walking backwards and forwards. I should call him—make him understand. I should hide—he couldn't see me like this!

Hegelina Fekkit and Old Mawde galloped to the gate, jostling at my side, curious.

"Who is it?"

"'Tis a Blackwood. I would recognise one of them anywhere."

"Aren't they cursed?"

"So the legend says."

"What is he doing in the sunlight then?"

"Why wouldn't he be?"

"If he's a nightwalker."

"He's not a nightwalker, you imbecile. That is the curse thrown to the Darkwoods of Craventhorpe."

"Who are you calling an imbecile, you derelict old crone!"

The cursed crones began to bicker between themselves, and I watched as Garrett, dressed in one of the dark suits he wore whilst on duty, knocked at the front door. He waited, knocked again, then stood back, scanning the windows. When the door remain closed, he walked to the side of the house furthest away from the field and disappeared from view. Minutes later he reappeared and walked across the back of the house.

"Shapeshifters! Idiot. They are cursed to walk the earth as shapeshifters."

"A gift!" exclaimed Hegelina.

"Stupid crone! How can being a shapeshifter be considered a gift? It is a curse. A torture."

"They are free!" she spat, her bitterness obvious. "They only have to live as beasts at the full moon whilst we … we are doomed to live as beasts until the evil crones that cursed us decide otherwise." She glared in my direction with narrowed eyes.

Old Mawde turned to stare at me too. "'Twas truly folly for Loveday to curse me," she threatened. "One day, one day very soon, I shall deliver her comeuppance!"

The women were bitter, and I couldn't blame them but wasn't willing to let them get away with threats to my aunts. "Hegelina has already tried that and look where it got her," I shot back.

"Pah! I nearly killed the old crone. I shall succeed the next time."

"There won't be a next time and if you do not watch your words, I shall suggest to Garrett Blackwood that roasted goat is very, very tasty, but that it tastes even better raw!" I glared at her with a meaningful stare, smiled as she shrank back, surprised at my own spirited retaliation, then turned to watch Garrett as he knocked at the kitchen door. When he received no answer, he opened the door and put a foot inside then called, "Hello! Anybody home?" He waited then took a step back whilst closing the door. The house was empty.

Old Mawde grunted. "Where are those crones?"

"They've gone out."

"That much is obvious."

"They went out in the dark, on their brooms. I watched them fly."

"And you let me suffer? Waiting each moment for them to step out of the kitchen?"

Hegelina cackled. "Yes!"

"If I weren't in so much discomfort I would headbutt you. In fact, I will."

Hegelina bent her head to the grass and snapped tombstone-like teeth around a cluster of dandelion leaves and pulled, unimpressed by the threat. Old Mawde continued to grumble.

My heart flipped. Garrett was walking towards us.

He leant against the gate. "Good afternoon, ladies," he said, looking at each of us in turn. "Now, I recognise Hegelina." He pointed to Hegelina. "And Old Mawde, but who are you?" He eyed me with curiosity, scanning my face and body. I moved to try and hide my udders from his gaze.

"She's your girlfriend!" Old Mawde crooned, her bleat ringing in the air.

Garrett continued to stare down at me. "Are you just a regular goat, or a cursed goat?" he asked. The question was rhetorical, he couldn't understand me anyway. I remained silent, avoiding eye contact, whilst Hegelina and Old Mawde continued to bleat at him, shouting out ineffective curses, berating him, and calling him names, none of which he understood.

"You're both vile!" I said during the break in the flow of some particularly salty language from Hegelina. They cackled in return. "I'm not surprised you've both been cursed to live as goats."

"Hah! And what about you little Miss Prissy Bloomers. Why are you cursed to live as a goat?"

"I'm not. It's just a transformation spell."

Hegelina's eyes narrowed, her interest piqued. "And why exactly have you been transformed into a goat then?"

It would be a mistake to tell them. "I don't know."

"Liar!"

"She is. She is a big, fat, and hairy liar!" crowed Old Mawde. Her eyes glittered. "With *huge* udders!" She was having fun.

"Well at least I won't be a goat for long. Unlike you!" I hit back. It was a pathetic effort at a comeback and both goats continued to cackle.

I realised then that Garrett was watching us with questioning bemusement. "So, you understand each other. Just how many cursed goats are the Haligern crones going to collect?

Where are they? Have you seen them?" He laughed. "No point talking to you, you can't tell me anyway." He leant against the fencepost, observing us. "I can't find Liv either. She's not in the shop and she's ignoring my calls."

Hegelina cackled. "Trouble in paradise!"

"She's right here!" Old Mawde cawed. "Your girlfriend's here."

Cackling erupted.

Garrett watched them with bemusement bordering on alarm then shook his head. Ringtones from his pocket claimed his attention and he pulled out his mobile then turned away, one finger in his ear. As he began to talk, pacing next to the fence, I trotted along beside him, listening.

"Speak up!" he demanded. "I'm outside and it's noisy." He listened. "Another attack? ... Oh, hell. Same location? ... Yes, I'm aware. Get a team ready. Forensics are on their way? ... Good. Do we have identification? ... Okay. Car? ... Okay. Well someone must know something. Walkers aren't usually that old. Check with the nursing homes—see if they're missing anyone. Check with social services too. They have lists of the vulnerable. There aren't that many women of that age in the village. If they're local, we should be able to name them quickly. And no press. Keep this one quiet. Two elderly women found mauled to death so soon after the last one will not go down well for us ... Right. I'll be there in half an hour. Meet me there."

"Is it the Beast?" I bleated. "Has he killed again?"

Garrett glanced down at me, frowned as he replaced his mobile, then strode back to his car.

"Did you hear that? He said two old women are dead."

"The Beast got them!"

Old Mawde cackled. "Ooh! It sounds like the Haligern crones have copped it!"

"Serves them right too!"

With a sickening feeling in the pit of my stomach I watched as Garrett stepped into his car. The Beast had struck again, and two elderly women were dead. With my aunts missing in suspicious circumstances I couldn't ignore the possibility that they were his victims.

Chapter Nineteen

As Garrett's car left the driveway, I clambered over the fence determined to follow and confront him.

"Come back!"

"You're not allowed to do that."

"She's done it."

As I galloped across the grass my hooves began to change and within seconds I was back to being the human version of me—sans clothes! I ran to the house, crouched and naked, and burst through the kitchen door. Four pairs of eyes looked at me with various levels of indifference.

"There you are! I've been waiting for your return. Breakfast was hours ago," Lucifer complained. Renweard rested his head back on his enormous paws, forlorn. Betsy tucked her head beneath a paw and returned to sleep, whilst Benny, Aunt Thomasin's raven familiar jumped down from the chair it had perched upon and hopped across the floor before flapping its wings and flying out of the door.

"I'll get you something in a minute, Lucifer."

"Please get dressed, Livitha. I'm beginning to feel queasy."

I ignored Lucifer's quip and grabbed Aunt Beatrice's apron from the hook and holding it against my body, ran upstairs to my bedroom. Within ten minutes I was back in my car, speeding through the narrow country lanes and hurtling out towards the moors, determined to face the Beast. As I motored closer, my bravado began to fail. How could I, a novice, very possibly delinquent witch, face-off with a monstrous killer?

With dark magick!

I stared into the road ahead. I couldn't use dark magick, could I?

It's the only way ... find the gypsy.

In my dazed state, still reeling from being cast as a goat, I listened to the inner voice. I should have questioned its source. I should have questioned its advice. Instead I did a three-point turn and headed back towards the field where the gypsies were parked.

Only minutes away, a bank of fog, the thickest I had seen this year, rolled in across the fields, its progress strangely rapid. Again, I took no notice of the unnatural speed and thickness of the mist and only pressed my foot to the accelerator, forcing the engine to work hard and propel me along the lane before the fog reached me. I failed and was quickly enveloped. Undeterred, headlights on, I slowed to a crawl and then pulled over to where I estimated the gypsy site to be and left the car. Despite the thickness of the fog, lights, hazed by the mist, shone from caravan windows and I stepped across the verge and into the field. The fog thickened and the lights disappeared but in the distance I could make out a figure walking towards me.

Too obscured to see clearly, I discerned the outline to be of a man. He appeared to be wearing a knee-length tunic with trousers beneath, and a furred mantle across his shoulders. A pair of antlers grew from his head, and, in his hand, he held a staff which he used to help propel him along. I recognised him instantly. Grimlock Yikkar! Without speaking, he continued towards me, tiny globules of light surrounding him like fireflies as he walked. Grimlock Yikkar worked for the Academy. Millicent was his boss. If he discovered why I was here, he would report me! I turned, hoping that he hadn't seen me, knowing instinctively that he was here because of me, and hurried back to my car, heart hammering, caught in the act of soliciting dark magick, feeling my way forward through the dense mist as though blind.

The car started with a chug and an unhealthy, phlegm-like growl and I pulled out back into the road. The fog miraculously cleared, and I turned back towards the direction of the moor, certain that I was now a doomed woman.

The morning had been bright with a chill breeze but as I motored to higher ground, grey clouds, almost black at their centre, gathered. A storm was brewing and although I knew that the weather on the moors could change rapidly, I was unprepared for what followed.

The road became steep, and my small car began to struggle. I took it down to second gear in an effort to climb a particularly steep hill, but it was slow going and I was relieved and surprised when it made it to the top. In the distance the farmhouse was visible and beyond it the ravine I'd walked through yesterday. A knot in the pit of my stomach tightened as I remembered the beast that had chased me but, determined to confirm my suspicions that two of my aunts had been attacked and lay dead, I convinced myself into believing that I could deal with him without the help of the gypsy's dark magick. My aunts had told me that my powers were strong and all I had to do was focus, so, I would focus, and the beast would be the one to combust. I would avenge the death of my aunts. Millicent could do whatever she wanted with me; I no longer cared.

But don't you need silver to kill a werewolf?

Yes, but I don't want to kill a werewolf.

Don't you? What about garlic?

No. That's vampires.
Wolfsbane?
That detects them.
Does it kill them?
I don't know!

My knowledge of werewolf lore had been gleaned from hours of watching films as a teenager and I realised that it ended at using a silver bullet to stop a werewolf. I did not have a bullet, or even a gun, and the only silver I owned had been handed over to the gypsy-witch. I slowed the car, mulling over the idea of trying a cloaking spell to use against Grimlock and return to the gypsy, then pulled over to the verge. If I went to her, I'd be fulfilling Millicent's prophecy and she had made it clear that using dark magick was punishable by death or exile and I was certain that she had sent Grimlock. Hadn't she said that they would be watching? Him turning up was proof that I was under surveillance. I dismissed the idea of returning to the gypsy and instead pulled out my mobile, hoping that a quick search on the internet would return information on how to deal with a werewolf other than with a silver bullet. In my defence, I wasn't thinking rationally and realise that the internet may not be the best place to search for that knowledge. My phone returned a blank screen—in this isolated location there was no signal. I threw the phone down on the seat in frustration then decided to continue onwards; I hadn't come here to kill the beast; I had come to discover the truth. I had coped with being attacked by an imp, I reassured myself, and would be able to use my new and improved powers to fend off a werewolf—if it made an appearance.

All around me bleak moorland stretched out to the horizon, the hills sitting black and undulating beneath the cloud-filled sky, and when they thickened, masking the sun, the day became a grim shade of grey.

I turned on the car's headlights, but they were of little use other than to warn other drivers of my presence of which there were none; like the landscape the roads were empty. However, where the road began to dip and twist, I felt sure that I would find a group of police vehicles and Garrett's car. During his phone conversation he had seemed to confirm that the bodies were close to where the walker had been found which was close to the ravine and the farmhouse. The house was behind me and the murder scene just along the road where it recovered from its dip and began to climb and twist again. I reached the bottom of the hill, followed the tight bend, and was faced with another steep hill.

The car chugged.

I took it down into second gear and powered it forward. Another chug was followed by a bang and then the engine cut dead. Smoke seeped from either side of the bonnet, and I watched it thicken.

With a sigh, too drained to respond with shock or concern, I retrieved the fire extinguisher from the boot and sprayed it at the bonnet. Flames flickered close to the windscreen and smoke billowed from beneath the car, my efforts useless. The car was about to be devoured.

And so are you!

With the mobile signal dead, there was nothing I could do apart from watch the smoke continue to thicken and grow black. I began to walk away, then quickened my pace, unsure if the fuel tank would explode and render me a fire ball too. Panic set in and I sprinted from the car but, with my breath coming hard and my thighs beginning to burn, I slowed. No explosion had thrown me off my feet, turned me into a fireball, or singed my brows, and I turned to look. Flames had begun to envelope the car and black smoke spiralled into the air where it was caught by the wind and blown into a dark smudge in the sky. Further down the road stood a dark figure obscured and warped by the flames.

The Beast!

My fingers tingled and with an eruption of rage, sparkling energy surrounded me. My hands shimmered and for the first time that morning I felt strong and knew that I was hidden from the creature. Let it stalk me. I was safe. What I wasn't safe from was the storm. As the sky darkened the wind picked up in strength, and I was buffeted, the open moorland offering no protection. With my shield of protection I began to climb the hill but became out of breath, my thighs burning with the effort of walking up the steep hill. Heart pounding, wishing I had kept up my efforts at powerwalking and lost the pounds of fat that clung around my waist, I reached the top. A biting wind blew harsher here and cold rain began to spatter light at first but quickly coming faster, landing as needles on my skin as the wind gusted.

Turning to check for the creature, I was relieved that it had disappeared. What was also absent was any sign of the police. I walked to the place where I had parked my car yesterday and followed my footsteps down the ravine, checking for the beast, but forcing myself onwards. There were two things on my mind. Firstly, the bodies may not be in the exact location, so I had to widen my search. Secondly, who was the man in the house and how did he know Garrett?

As I continued further into the moors, and as the weather took a turn for the worse, I had to find shelter. The rain turned to sleet, soaking through my fleece, and I became increasingly wet and cold despite my shield of magick.

I emerged from the ravine, scanned the landscape for the Beast, then made my way to the house where light shone from the window. It spurred me on but growing fatigued from the effort of keeping the shield intact, and increasingly cold, I slowed, grew lightheaded, my hands beginning to shake as my blood sugar dipped. With my energy levels crashing, the protective shield waned and, as I slumped against a rocky outcrop, it faded then died. "Just taking a break," I sighed. "I'll be alright in a minute."

The wind continued to whip at my face, sharp and icy.

I began to despair.

It had been a bad idea to come out onto the moors, but I was full of bad ideas and now two of my aunts were dead! It was my fault they had come up onto the moors to find the Beast. If I hadn't got involved with Garrett none of this would have happened. If two were dead, where were the other two? Did the Beast have them captive? Were they hiding somewhere on the moors afraid of being spotted by him? I groaned, the pain in my conscience as great as the pain of fatigue that was swamping my body. I should have told them about the gypsy's warning and then they wouldn't be dead! It was all my fault.

Several minutes passed as the wind, rain, and my inner voice continued to punish me, dragging me down into a trough of self-pity, but with the weather now a greater threat to my life than the Beast, I made a last, desperate effort, to reach the cottage.

Progress was slow, the strength in my legs almost gone, but at last I reached the cottage door, bedraggled, half frozen, and without hope. If the beast attacked me now, I had no energy left to fend it off. I grasped the knocker and rapped at the door.

Chapter Twenty

The man who opened the door took my breath away. At over six foot tall with broad shoulders and dark hair, he was almost the mirror image of Garrett. His hair was wet and his breathing heavy—as though he had just run in from the rain. He stared at me for several moments, dark caramel eyes scrutinizing mine.

"My car broke down," I gasped whilst leaning against the storm porch. "And I have no signal on my phone. Do you have one I can use, please?"

He opened the door to allow me to pass. "Come in."

I staggered inside and was instantly enveloped by warmth. The door opened directly into the living room and, although sparsely decorated, it was a pleasant room. A fire burned in the hearth, and a table lamp filled the room with mellow light. A large sofa, its dark leather softened and cracked by age and use, sat before the fire, a sheepskin thrown over its back. A knitted blanket lay over an arm.

"You're wet," he stated. "I'll get you a blanket. The phone is on the table, Help yourself." He gestured to a console table beside the door.

"Thanks. You look a little wet yourself," I stated, despite my fatigue.

He frowned, taken aback. "I've been out to get more logs for the fire," he pointed to the hearth where a large wicker basket was filled with logs, some spattered with rain. "You're welcome to sit down and warm up. I'll make you a cup of tea, or would you prefer coffee? I have hot chocolate?"

Thankful for his kindness to me, a bedraggled stranger he could have turned away from the door, I settled on a hot chocolate, and moved towards the fire.

"Best let me have your fleece. It looks sodden."

I passed him the fleece and he handed me the blanket from the arm of the sofa.

"Make your call, then sit down and get warm. I won't be long."

He disappeared through a door and after calling roadside rescue, who promised to be at the scene within two hours, I seated myself close to the fire. Noises of a kettle beginning to heat its water was joined by the clink of mugs and the opening of a fridge. Minutes later he returned and passed me a mug of steaming hot chocolate. It tasted rich and sweet. Its warmth was soothing and, laced with sugar, it revived my energy. Although on edge, and sitting with a stranger, I no longer felt vulnerable.

Whilst I sat, he stood beside the fire, one arm on the mantel. "So," he said, "You're not a walker, which begs the question, how come you're this far out on the moor?"

"My car broke down."

"Ah."

"It set on fire."

"Oh!"

"I think it may still be on fire."

"Not a good start to your morning!" he stated dryly.

"Nope." I took another sip of the sweet hot chocolate, delighting in its smooth warmth. "This is good!" I said.

"It came in a hamper at Yu ... Christmas."

So, he celebrated Yule—a pagan then. I eyed him with renewed interest.

"Did you get through?" he asked. "To report your car?"

"Yes, they'll be here within the hour. I'll go back to the car and wait there."

"That's not a good idea," he said. "The moors are a dangerous place for a woman on her own."

I caught glimpses of Garrett in the man's face as mine began to warm. Coming out of the cold and into the warmth always made the blood rush to my cheeks and I could feel the flush intensifying. I took another sip of chocolate then decided to press ahead and find out as much about him as I could. However, as I opened my mouth to speak, he began his own interrogation.

"So, why are you here?"

"I broke down. My car set on fire," I repeated.

"Yes, but why are you here?"

"I was on the way to work-"

"Work? Over the moors. Surely there are quicker routes? Isn't this out of your way?"

"Well, yes," I replied to his quickly fired questions.

"So, you took a detour across the moor. Strange behaviour. What's your name?"

"Alice ... Yikkar," I lied. Hers was the first name that came to mind.

He frowned. "Alice Yikkar?"

I nodded.

The frown deepened. "I see."

"And yours?"

"Finn."

We were now both wary of the other. It was my turn to bombard him with questions.

"So, Finn, have you lived here long?"

"Some time."

"I thought the house was abandoned." I waited for him to respond but he remained silent, and I began to feel unnerved by his gaze. "So, do you like it?"

"It's a desolate and barren place. It serves me well."

"Don't you get lonely ... out here, on your own?"

He threw me a sideways glance. "No."

Tension increased in the room. "Do you sometimes see ... walkers?"

"Too many recently. And far too many curious women."

The flush on my cheeks tingled and I felt the fizz in my fingers relight as my energy returned, anxiety making my inner magick grow turbulent. I pressed on.

"They say a woman was killed here."

"No one was killed here!"

"There was a murder just beyond the ravine."

"That's not here."

"No, but it's close. They say a wild animal killed her—a beast."

He held my gaze for a moment. "People have wild imaginations. It's more likely to be a psychopath. It's happened before around here."

"Yes, in the exact place too."

"So?"

"So it could be the same killer. He's been let out of prison. Or a copycat killer? Or ... the Beast?"

He rolled his eyes. "What beast?"

"The Beast of Wolfstane Moor."

"That's what they called the guy who murdered those women in the 80s, isn't it?"

"It is, but there was a beast that killed on these moors years before that."

"Then he'd be dead, surely."

"He would be very, very old."

"Too old to do any harm, I'd say. It's more likely a copycat killer. These desolate places often attract lunatics. The moor has a peculiar effect on people. It's why they build asylums for the criminally insane on them; bad places run by bad people." He stared into the fire.

"Do you mean like Broadmoor?" My stomach churned. Garrett had mentioned an escapee from the prison.

"Yes." His answer was curt.

The tension in the room increased.

I had to know about my aunts. "I heard, this morning, that another two women had been found dead. Close to where the other woman was murdered. It's close to here—again."

His eyes locked to mine, the caramel of his eyes flashing orange as they caught the reflection of the fire. He took a sip from his mug. "Then it seems that this place is very dangerous—for women. Maybe even more so for the curious ones."

I swallowed against a dry throat; there was something dangerous in the glint in his eye.

"Tell me again, Alice Yikkar, why you are so far away from home?"

"I told you, my car broke down."

"That may be true, but why are you here? Why did you drive so far out of your way? And why have you lied about your name? It's definitely not Alice Yikkar." His eyes flashed and he took a step towards me.

I had made a terrible mistake.

He towered over me. I stood up, took a sideways step, and ran for the door. He got there first and grabbed the handle. I stepped away from him and back into the room.

"Tell me who you are, and this time tell truth. I know Alice Yikkar is dead. So unless you are a ghost, you're lying."

"You know who she is?"

He nodded.

I noticed then the elongated canines at the sides of his mouth. "You're the Beast!"

He smiled. "I am. Now, who are you?"

There was no point in lying. "Livitha Erickson."

For a second, he seemed taken aback and then a glint appeared in his eyes. "Daughter of Soren Erickson," he finished.

"How ... how do you know that?"

"There's a lot I know."

"You killed my aunts!"

"Your aunts?"

"The two women you killed on the moor!"

He grunted but a smile curved onto his lips. "They deserved it."

"What! How can you say that? They were the sweetest women that ever lived. Beautiful, special-"

His eyes locked to mine. "They were conniving and devious."

"You're a liar!" I shouted. "They were neither of those things."

His eyes narrowed. "It was kill or be killed," he said in ominous tones.

"If they wanted to kill you then they had good reason. I think being the Beast of Wolfstane Moor is good enough reason!"

As he glared down at me, amber eyes glinting, the door swung open, knocking into his back. With his attention on the intruder, I moved back towards the fire, readying myself for confrontation.

Garrett stood in the doorway. "Liv! What are you doing here?"

"Her car broke down—she says!"

"What are *you* doing here?" I countered.

"I've come to see my cousin."

"Your cousin? This monster is your cousin?"

Garrett shut the door behind him. "Monster?" He threw a glance at Finn. "He can be ... difficult at times, but a monster?" He stepped further into the room. "Let me introduce you properly. Finn, this is Liv."

"Nice to meet you, Liv. Garrett has told me a lot about you."

"He has?"

"Yes. In fact, it's difficult to get him to shut up about you."

"Oh!" I glanced from Garrett to Finn, noticing the similarities between them. "Anyway, this is all just a distraction. Garrett arrest him! He's admitted to killing my aunts."

Garrett frowned. "What have you been telling her, Finn?"

He shrugged. "Just my way of getting through the day." The man began to laugh. "She was so in earnest. I couldn't help myself."

"What's going on?"

"My cousin thinks he is being funny."

"It's not a joke. My aunts are dead!"

"What makes you think that?"

"You said that two elderly women had been killed."

"Yes, but they're not your aunts. I can confirm that."

"Are you sure?"

"Yes, I'm sure. They've already been identified. I've just come from the scene. They weren't local either." He frowned. "But how do you know that the women had been killed? It was only reported a few hours ago?"

"I heard you on the phone."

"When did you hear me on the phone?"

I knew then he was about to realise that I had been one of the goats. He pressed his lips together, eyes widening, attempted to suppress a laugh, and snorted as he failed.

"You were the third goat!"

"No!" I lied. We locked eyes. I tried to brazen it out. Finn watched.

"You were."

Mortification rose to my cheeks as a painful, heated, prickling. Garrett had seen me as a goat, my udders swinging beneath me.

"I was in the woods," I tried.

He shook his head. "Too far away. Try again."

Finn continued to watch our conversation with fascination, a smile stuck at the corner of his mouth.

"Well, I-"

Garrett burst out laughing.

"It's not funny! It was the worst experience of my life!" I complained. "Hegelina and Old Mawde are just ... horrible people and I had to spend the entire night in that pen. It was cold and windy, and I was hungry! Stop laughing! I had to sleep on straw."

Our eyes met. "So," he snorted again, "did they milk you?"

Finn burst out laughing "What!"

I batted Garrett's arm, my cheeks now burning, and strode to the fire, wanting distance between us. As I watched the flames dance, my cheeks burning with mortification, a hand lay heavily on my shoulder and then Garrett's arm slipped across my back. "I'm sorry, Liv. It must have been awful."

I nodded but didn't speak.

"And ... and you had some lovely udders!" Again laughter broke out and I batted his shoulder once more. His arms wrapped around me. "Sorry," he said whilst holding me tight. "I couldn't help it."

"And you tell me off for having a sense of humour," Finn laughed.

For those moments, I put aside my anger at his impending fatherhood. "It's so embarrassing," I said, my words muffled as I pressed against his chest. "What's going on, Garrett? Where are my aunts?"

Chapter Twenty-One

Relieved that my aunts weren't dead, the pain and resentment returned, and I gently pulled myself from Garrett's embrace. He may be ignoring the elephant in the room, but I wasn't. I wasn't ready to talk about his pregnant girlfriend, but I couldn't pretend that she hadn't turned up and destroyed all of my future hopes either.

Emotions bubbling close to the surface, I managed to blink away tears that were hazing my vision and made a pretence of moving to the fire to get warm. My hair was beginning to dry, and I took a sip of chocolate wishing it had my aunt's calming elixir in it.

The conversation turned to Finn. He was a cousin, the son of one of Uncle Tobias' brothers, working on a complex project, and had asked Garrett if he could stay at the farmhouse, a quiet place where he could focus on work and pull his ideas together.

"It's very inconvenient, having all these people being murdered," he said with a dry tone and a wry smile. "I haven't had a day without interruption."

"Very inconsiderate of them," I returned. "Perhaps we can ask the Beast to kill his victims out of sight of the farmhouse."

He laughed and glanced over to Garrett. "You're right, she is quirky."

"Thanks," I said.

"In a good way. We like quirky, don't we Gar."

Garrett nodded.

"What's the project you're working on?"

"It's not something I can talk about, I'm afraid, but it involves corruption. I'm working with a number of whistle-blowers and pretty sure I'm close to being able to present my findings to the Council."

Garrett flashed him a warning look.

"You work for the Council?" I said, immediately thinking of our local council. It didn't surprise me to hear there was corruption there; it was common knowledge that the large construction firms often got the planning permission they asked for even if the land was on the green belt or agricultural land. And then there was the case of the councillor who had been found committing fraud. Add to that a number of MPs in the area who had suddenly accumulated wealth far greater than their yearly government salary and it was obvious the upper echelons were inhabited by criminals.

"No, I work for a firm of forensic accountants."

"Ah!"

"He's a data analyst," Garrett filled in. "Works uncovering fraud, money laundering, that kind of thing. He's brilliant. When our guys are stumped, we turn to him."

They exchanged smiles.

"We do … sensitive work," Finn added. "Not something I can talk about."

"I see." It was intriguing and explained why he was staying at the farmhouse, to an extent. "It must be very … complex, if you're willing to stop out here all on your own."

"It suits me. I may come more often."

"You're always welcome," Garrett responded. "The place is yours as long as you need it."

"Thanks!"

Garrett checked his watch. "Right, well, I'll have to be getting back to work; people being murdered brings with it a ton of paperwork. Liv, do you need a lift? I saw your car out on the road."

"I've called roadside rescue. They'll be here soon. I can wait."

Garrett shook his head. "No, I'll take you home."

"I need to find my aunts," I said.

"I'm pretty sure they can take care of themselves, Liv. It's not as if they're your typical elderly relatives, is it."

"True," I replied.

"The Haligern crones?" Finn asked. "I'd say they're more than capable of taking care of themselves. Is Loveday still as beautiful as she was? It's been a good few years since I saw them."

"You know my aunts?"

"Know of them. I've been to a few gatherings where they were present. There's certainly something special about them. They're a cut above most of the crones I've come across."

I appreciated his words. They did reassure me but my aunts not being home to milk Old Mawde made me fear the worst. "I know they're capable and all that, but it's not like them to be out all night. Something could have happened to them."

"I'm sure they'll turn up when they're ready," Garrett placated. "They're probably not even around here."

"I guess, but I had to see if it was them the Beast had attacked."

Garrett sighed. "I understand, but Liv, I don't want you out here on the moor alone. I'd be much happier if you'd let me take you back home or to the shop. In fact, I insist. Roadside recovery can take your car to the local garage."

Still damp from the earlier downpour, I had no real desire to wait by the car and clouds were already moving back across the sun holding the threat of more rain, and so I agreed.

Minutes later I was seated next to Garrett, travelling back across the moor. The sun that had peeked through the thinning clouds had disappeared and the sky was dark. Fat raindrops began to fall as we turned onto the road.

"Looks like a storm is brewing," Garrett said as we wound down another steep road.

"It does," I said spotting a plume of dark smoke in the distance, "but at least it'll help put my car out."

He laughed. "Always a silver lining, aye, Liv?"

"You've got to see the bright side," I returned. "I'm just glad it's not summer. It could've set the moor alight."

"Hmm, we definitely don't want another wildfire."

The last thing I wanted was to talk to Garrett about his pregnant ex, so the banal and stilted conversation continued for several more minutes until we came across the smouldering and burned-out husk of my car. "You weren't joking about the fire!"

"I can't believe it burned so fast!"

"I don't think roadside rescue are going to want to take it quite yet."

As we took a slow drive past the wreck, the rescue truck appeared. Garrett slowed to a stop and we both got out to talk to the mechanic. He agreed to collect the car tomorrow once it had had time to cool. Garrett took a reel of white tape and stakes from the boot of his car and placed a barricade around the burned-out car. 'Police Aware', printed in blue lettering, fluttered in the wind.

I asked Garrett to take me back to the shop. Despite the intrigue and upheaval of the past days I determined to carry on as normal as far as possible. Throwing myself into work would help dull the pain I felt at how badly my relationship with Garrett was disintegrating. The previous evening he had tried to call me twice and sent a single text message. I had ignored them all. It was cowardly of me, I know, but I wasn't ready to talk to him and have that conversation where he let me go. I knew how it would end; he'd insist that he loved me, but he was a man of honour, and his responsibility was towards the child he had fathered. He would be getting married and trying to make the best of it. We could still be friends and he'd always love me, but he was duty bound and would disgrace his family if he didn't take the woman in. My heart hurt as I ruminated on this imagined conversation, Garrett silent beside me.

As we approached the village boundary, Garrett began to speak. "Liv, about the other day ..."

"If you're going to talk about what happened at afternoon tea, then please don't. I'm not ready."

"But-"

"Please, Garrett!"

"Liv, let me explain."

"My aunts are missing, and women are being murdered. I think we've both got other things we need to sort out before we can ... before we can talk about that."

He sighed and the remainder of the journey was silent. We drew up outside the shop and I got out. "Thanks for the lift."

"Liv!"

"Yes?"

"I'll call you later."

"Okay." I began to close the door.

"Liv!"

"Yes?"

"I love you. Don't forget that."

The sadness in his voice made my heart ache. I managed to nod, not trusting my voice to betray my emotion, and stepped into the shop as he pulled away from the kerb.

Chapter Twenty-Two

As I stepped inside, noise far louder than any fairy could make, came from one of the backrooms and I realised that the shop door had been unlocked! I listened for several more moments then stepped further inside.

My heart skipped a beat.

The noise of clinking as bottles were knocked together was accompanied by a trilling song and the shuffle of feet.

Aunt Beatrice!

Emotion overwhelmed me and tears began to flow.

"Why, whatever's the matter child?" Standing in the back-room doorway, a box in her arms, she frowned with concern. I had never seen a more beautiful sight! "You're crying!"

I nodded then managed, "I am."

Aunt Beatrice placed the box on the side and swept forward, wrapping her arms around me. Petite and inches shorter than me, her embrace was surprisingly strong, and I was a child again. "Now, now. No need for tears. Tell Aunty Bea all about it? Is it that policeman again?"

"No! I'm just so glad to see you!" I rasped. "More women were killed yesterday, and I thought it was you!"

Now openly sobbing, she led me to the chair behind the counter. "Why ever would you think I was dead?"

"Because you weren't at home and Old Mawde was complaining about not being milked! And the curtains weren't drawn open." I rambled. "And Garrett couldn't find you. And he said that two elderly women had been found dead on the moors!"

"There, there. I told Loveday that we should have told you, but everything happened in such a hurry!"

"Are you all ... alive?"

"Of course we are, child! It takes more than the Beast of Wolfstane Moor to defeat a Haligern crone. And besides, he's a softie at heart."

With her arm across my shoulder, I began to calm down, shocked at the outburst of pain that had overwhelmed me. Relief began to flow, and Aunt Beatrice offered to make a cup of tea. I asked for some of Aunt Thomasin's calming elixir. She chuckled and disappeared into the kitchenette.

I found a piece of tissue in my pocket and used that to wipe away my tears then realised what she had said. "What do you mean that the Beast of Wolfstane Moor is a softie? How can a killer who rips his victim to shreds be a softie?"

The kettle drowned out my call and so I waited for her return before repeating my question.

"So, have you met him?"

"The Beast?"

"Oh, yes. Many years ago. Decades, actually."

"But if he's here killing again, how can you call him a softie?"

"Oh, I wasn't talking about that Beast."

"There's more than one?"

She nodded. "It's confusing, I know, but the problem is that any killer around here gets called the Beast. Take the man who killed those women when you were a teenager, they called him the Beast, and now the killer whose at it again, they're calling him the Beast too. The Beast I knew lived such a long time ago. Cursed, poor man, to live as a werewolf when the moon was full, but he left this area at the turn of last century. Or, at least, there were no sightings of him. Did you know that there used to be a parade on All Hallows? The locals would dress up as werewolves and march through the village. The idea was to scare the werewolf off."

"Did it work?"

"Well, there were no sightings during those years. But I think it more likely that he moved out of the area or was killed—though no one ever claimed that." She sighed then laughed. "Ah, the days that I have seen, Livitha." She took a sip of tea, and I took a sip of mine. "There's only a few drops. You're getting far too fond of the elixir to my thinking."

"It helps," I said.

"Hmm, well better to rely on your own inner strength. It doesn't do to become too dependent on ... substances."

"You make me sound like an addict!"

She shook her head. "Don't take it the wrong way, dear. I'm only trying to help."

I took another sip of tea, enjoying the flow of easing warmth the elixir brought. It took the edge off my frayed nerves and turned the volume down on the waves of sadness I felt each time I thought of Garrett.

"Now, there's plenty to do. I've brought some more of Aunt Thomasin's lip balm and Aunt Euphemia has made a new batch of the moisturiser."

"The one with wild pansy?"

"Yes."

"Oh, good. That sells really well. We've had great feedback about it."

Aunt Beatrice smiled then noticed the box I had filled for Neil Montpellier sitting on the counter. "It's for Karyn Montpellier. Her husband came in the other day and asked for help. She's very stressed about the killings."

"Her father was the policeman who caught the man who killed those women when you were a teenager, I think."

"He was," I agreed. "And she's up in arms because the man has been let out of jail. Her husband seems to be getting the brunt of her temper. He thinks she's going through the change too but thinks he'll get his head bitten off if he broaches the subject."

"She is a fiery one," Aunt Beatrice agreed.

"He asked me to give her the gift box from Haligern Apothecary on the pretext that it was her birthday and that we're thanking her for all the work she's done for the village."

"Well, she was the one who helped us get the planning permission through. So much corruption there, Livitha, but she helped us. Or at least – we approached the right councillor to bribe." She followed this revelation with a cackle.

"I hate to deceive this way, but he seemed so upset about his wife's struggles that I agreed to the ruse and promised to deliver the box myself."

"It seems plausible enough. Why don't you take it now? Get some fresh air and clear your mind."

"I guess I could."

"I can hold the fort whilst you go."

With the box prettily arranged and wrapped, I set off for Karyn Montpellier's home, a five-minute walk from the shop. Thankfully, the clouds that had brought the rain had been swept along by the wind and, although it was cold, it remained dry.

The house was one of the oldest in the village, a seventeenth century cottage built of stone. With sash windows and a shingled porch with trellis either side it was a quaint and pleasing sight. Entered through a wooden porch with apex roof, a stone slabbed path led to the front door. Either side the garden was set to lawn with the traditional borders of flowers. At this time of year the garden was mostly green, but in the summer, it was a haven of brightly coloured foxgloves, peonies, crocosmia and irises.

Karyn answered the door with a smile. She recognised me immediately and after a quick explanation as to why I was on her doorstep, invited me in. As she led me through to the kitchen, I took note of the numerous photographs hung on the hallway walls. Most appeared to be of family and friends. There were images of holidays filled with smiling faces and people dressed in shorts, squinting against the sun, or wearing sunglasses. A couple showed Karyn skiing. There were several of her and her husband holding up pheasants in one hand, a broken gun hung on the crook of their arms. Another was of them clay pigeon shooting. Another showed them on the moors, a springer spaniel at their sides, again with disarmed guns hanging at the crook of their arms. At least three showed Karyn dressed in running gear, set to the backdrop of a particularly rocky area of the moors, receiving an award. Some were of a man in police uniform standing proudly beside a woman. In black and white and given the car they stood beside, and the woman's clothes, they dated from the sixties or early seventies. There were more of the same man as he aged, some photographs of him receiving awards. I presumed that this was her father, PC Ernest Idle. There were several of parties, some dated by the guests' clothes to the sixties, seventies, and eighties. One was of a Hallowe'en party, the group appearing in the typical costumes: witches, vampires, zombies, vampire brides, and werewolves. Most interestingly, there was one of the parade Aunt Beatrice had mentioned. I stopped to look.

"This is fascinating," I said pointing to the image. It was a strange sight. A dozen men dressed in homemade werewolf-like costumes some beating drums, others holding pan lids to clash as cymbals, several carrying pitchforks, were led by a tall man, again dressed as a werewolf. He held before him a banner depicting a man pointing a gun at a slain werewolf.

"Do you remember the parades?" she asked. It was a reasonable question; we were the same age.

I shook my head. "I don't think we ever attended."

"The last one was the year before the Beast of Wolfstane Moor killed that girl. You must remember that. We were at school together when it happened."

"Oh, yes, I do remember that, just not the parade."

"Oh, it was wonderful." She pointed to a young girl in the crowd. "That's me. The head werewolf is my dad, may his soul rest in peace."

"He was a good man."

She nodded. "Thank you, yes, he was. The best. She stroked the image of her father behind the glass. "That year was so much fun. We had a bonfire. My mother and her friends had baked potatoes. The whole village was there. It was so atmospheric." She sighed. "The killer put a stop to that."

"Such a shame," I commiserated.

"Yes. My father had taken up the job of organising it but when the killings happened, I don't think he could stomach it anymore and no one else picked up the reins. I really wanted to get it going again, but with these deaths ... well, it would be in poor taste."

"Perhaps in the future?"

"Perhaps. Come through to the kitchen, I'll make you a cup of tea."

Although there were dark circles beneath her eyes, and she seemed weary, Karyn didn't appear to be overly stressed. However, I wanted to help her, and her husband, so agreed to the cup of tea, ready to explain the products I'd packed into the gift hamper, hopefully without triggering offence.

As the kettle boiled, she turned her attention to the gift box. I watched with apprehension as she picked out the first jar of anti-ageing cream. "I definitely need this!" she said with a polite smile.

I realised then that everything in the box was geared towards ageing and the menopause and that I should have put something 'neutral' in there too. "I packed it myself. We're the same age, so I thought I'd pack it with things that I've found useful. This time in our lives can be tough."

She glanced at me. "Do you mean women of a 'certain' age?"

"I'm fifty, so I guess so," I replied warily. Was this where she took offence?

She lifted out the vintage bottle of calming elixir and held it to the light. "Oh, this is beautiful. The red glass sparkles. Is it vintage? I love the cork stopper."

"It is a vintage bottle. We do refills at the shop, so just bring it back when it's empty and we'll top it up again," I said. "I put a few drops in a cup of tea when I'm feeling a little on edge—you know, when my hormones start playing up."

"Oh, yes, I know!" she said with a laugh.

The tension eased and we drank tea whilst talking about the jars of cream, lotions, and potions and what they could be used for.

"You're so clever, Liv!"

"Oh, I don't know about that. My aunts have decades of knowledge. They're the ones behind this really, I'm just trying to run the show."

"I'll have to pop in and take a look. I'm so sorry I missed the opening. It was a blast from what I heard. Very clever dramatics!"

I remembered the open evening where the event had begun to spiral out of control as a brawl had erupted and then Vlad's three new and delinquent wives had appeared complete with their vampire designer dog. Thankfully, the guests had thought it was all part of the opening and enjoyed the spectacle although there were a few who had been spooked and left.

"It was fun," I said.

"Great PR."

I nodded, unwilling to explain the truth behind the event.

As she sipped the tea, I noticed several deep scratches on her hands and wrists. Some looked red as though on the verge of infection. She noticed my glance. "I love gardening," she said. "Had a fight with a particularly thorny rose!"

"They look sore. We have a salve that could help heal them."

"I have some antiseptic in the cupboard though it would be good to have something natural."

I smiled but found her explanation hard to believe; the damage to her skin looked as though she'd fallen into the thorns and then fought her way out. "You know where we are. I'd love to see you at the shop."

Again she smiled. As she took another sip of tea, I noticed two more things. The first was the werewolf costume hanging on the washing line in the back garden and the other was three frames, each featuring a newspaper story.

Again, she caught my glance. "Old Wolfy's on the line! That was my father's costume—the one he wore in those photographs in the hallway. I've been clearing out the garage and found it in an old trunk. It had a mildewy whiff." Tears pricked her eyes. "Poor dad, he'd be turning in his grave right now—well, if he weren't cremated." She reached for a tissue from the Welsh dresser behind the table and wiped at her tears.

"Because of the Beast?"

She nodded. "Yes! They've let him out of prison—on a technicality!" There was a note of hysteria in her voice. "It's just so wrong! They're wrong! The Beast is back killing women and they let him out on a technicality! They should be investigating *him* and not my dad! And Heather would be alive too!"

"I'm so sorry to hear that," I commiserated.

"Heather Norton was a close family friend. It really is heart-breaking that she died at the hands of the monster my father helped put away. It's criminal!"

"Do you really think that the Beast, the one who killed the women when we were teens, has come back? Wouldn't he be old now? I mean, it was more than thirty years ago."

"Thirty-six years. And yes, I think he would although the police don't want to entertain the idea—they're more interested in blaming my father."

"They think your father was the killer?"

"No! They ... they think there were discrepancies with the original evidence. But my father was the best of men—hard working and loyal. He was *not* a bent copper!" She looked at me with imploring, bloodshot eyes.

"No, of course not."

"DCI Blackwood could sort this out. I've tried talking to him, but he just fobs me off." She looked at me in a moment of revelation. "But you could talk to him, couldn't you?"

"Erm-"

"You're his girlfriend. Aren't you?" Her words held the tone of accusation.

"Well ... we're friends, yes. I've known him since we were teenagers."

"Of course! You were sweet on each other at school."

I managed a wry smile. "We were."

"Then please, try to make him see sense. My father was a good man! He would have followed the letter of the law—it's the kind of policeman he was, and he won awards for his work, so that proves he was a good policeman too."

"Well, I'm not sure there's much I can do," I said. "Garrett's job is not really any of my business."

She sighed and looked at the framed newspaper reports. "I know. I'm sorry. I'm just so upset that my father's name should be dragged through the mud like this especially now that he's not here to defend himself."

"I'm so sorry, Karyn. I'll share your concerns with DCI Blackwood but perhaps it's best to let the investigation run its course. At the end, I'm sure, everything will be alright." I had no idea if that were true or not but given that Karyn seemed on the verge of hysteria, I didn't want to fan those flames.

"Thank you, Liv. I'm sorry for the outburst. These are difficult times."

"They are and I do understand. Try the elixir, a few drops in your tea a couple of times a day when you're feeling particularly stressed. It works wonders. I use it myself."

"I will."

As I rose to leave, the front door opened.

"Karyn, I'm home!"

"Ah, Neil's back."

With the werewolf costume flapping in the background, its fang-filled and hairy mask staring blindly into the kitchen, the couple embraced, and I was struck by how similar they were. Both were tall and slim and of a similar height and build, Neil only marginally broader than his wife—one of those odd couples who had chosen their doppelganger as their partner in life.

Chapter Twenty-Three

That night I ignored Garrett's efforts to call me. It was childish and cowardly, but I just couldn't face *that* conversation. I needed some time to process the end of our relationship so that when he explained the inevitable, I was at least a little shielded from the emotional fallout. Also, I didn't trust my ability to contain my magick and feared the resulting unhappiness could spark an emotionally charged implosion; I was already struggling to suppress the tingling in my fingers and had had to put out a few embers that had strayed to the wrapping paper on the counter at the shop. Aunt Beatrice had complained about the black marks, thrown me a worried glance, then mumbled something about working on my education and making a new batch of elixir.

The following morning, after a restless, sweat-filled night where dreams had morphed into nightmares and the werewolf I'd seen on the moors appeared at my bedroom window, tapping to be let in, I woke to Lucifer asleep on my belly and a keen need to know exactly where my aunts had been whilst they were missing and what they had been up to. Their explanation had been vague verging on obfuscation, and they hadn't presented a coherent front, so I showered and dressed, determined to tease the truth out of them.

However, on reaching the kitchen I was confronted by the excited tones of Mrs. Driscoll sharing the latest gossip.

"And do you know that only yesterday this article came out suggesting that poor old PC Idle was the killer." She waved the rolled-up newspaper gripped in her hand.

"I didn't know," Aunt Euphemia replied as I stepped into the kitchen.

"It was! Just dreadful to suggest he was the killer when he can't defend himself and this new murder – oh, poor Mrs. Benson – proves that he wasn't. It was the Beast! He's back. And now he's attacking us in the village!" Mrs. Driscoll appeared to sway and then sat down heavily in a chair.

My aunts exchanged glances.

"This really is very dreadful," said Aunt Thomasin.

"Indeed," agreed Aunt Beatrice. "Livitha, be a dear and fetch a cup and saucer for Mrs. Driscoll. She's had a terrible shock."

I fetched the teacup and saucer then poured Mrs. Driscoll a cup of tea whilst Aunt Beatrice laced it with the calming elixir.

"Not too much, Beatrice," whispered Aunt Thomasin. "This batch has extra oomph, on behalf of Livitha's issues."

A single drop was allowed to fall and then the drink placed in front of Mrs. Driscoll who appeared dazed.

"There now, take a sip, and tell us all about it."

As instructed, Mrs. Driscoll sipped her tea, sighed as the soothing concoction began to do its work then released the newspaper. I picked it up. Across the front, written in large black type, was 'The Beast: Uncovered'. Below it was a photograph of PC Idle and beside that was a photograph, dressed in prison uniform and looking unkempt and miserable, of the man imprisoned for the murders on the moors. As Mrs. Driscoll continued to drink her tea, I began to read through the article. It was a lurid exposé of a less than flattering overview of PC Idle's career and personal life. There were details of investigations of corruption and bribery that had been quashed but never fully examined along with adulterous liaisons. There was a connection too with Leonard Dimmock, the supposed killer, a man, the journalist claimed, who had damning evidence of PC Idle's criminal activity. It went on to suggest that PC Idle had silenced his accusers and bribed officials to quash the investigations into his wrongdoing and then framed the man who held the evidence against him. At the end, it claimed, there was evidence to suggest that PC Idle was linked to the murders on the moors and that the main witness to his corruption had died only last week in suspicious circumstances upon the very moor the original murders had taken place.

"Who is the 'main witness'?" I asked.

Aunt Thomasin leant over to look at the newspaper as I pointed to the text. "It must be one of the women who died on the moors recently. I don't know of any other deaths on the moors."

"Hmm."

"It's a scandal that they let people publish rubbish like this. Poor Karyn is beside herself. But this new murder – poor Jane ..." Mrs. Driscoll pulled back a sob, "proves ... proves it beyond reasonable doubt that Leonard Dimmock is the Beast of Wolfstane Moor and everything they are saying about PC Idle is wrong. Poor Karyn. But she's coming back fighting!"

"She is?"

"Yes, she's talking about holding a rally in the village—to protest Leonard Dimmock's release. And now, after what happened this morning, I think it'll happen. People are scared."

I glanced at my watch. It was only nine am but with the village being such a tightknit community it didn't surprise me that word had spread so fast.

"Where was Jane Benson killed?"

"That's the worst thing! On the outskirts of the village. Basil Rathstone found her this morning – poor man!"

"So close!"

"Yes! And he said she'd been horribly attacked. He's a gentleman so wouldn't divulge, but if she was in a state like the others then she had been ... Oh, I can't say it."

"Shredded?"

Mrs. Driscoll nodded her head whilst holding a tissue to her nose with trembling fingers. Aunt Thomasin placed a hand on her shoulder. Mrs. Driscoll was milking the event for all that it was worth.

"I'm thinking of going away for a few weeks. It doesn't feel safe around here now."

"How old was Mrs. Benson?" I asked.

"Oh, she was in her late seventies."

"And what was she doing in the lane?"

"Walking her dog, Henry."

"Another murder in the morning?"

Mrs. Driscoll nodded. "Just like the others! But this one ... so close to home! I'm only surprised I didn't hear her scream—it's that close to my house!"

"Take another sip of tea, dear," Aunt Beatrice said in soothing tones. She caught my gaze and rolled her eyes. "It's all very distressing, we know."

"It is."

With Mrs. Driscoll in a calmer state my aunts pored over the article whilst I ate a breakfast of freshly baked bread thickly buttered and dolloped with marmalade. Efforts at reducing my waistline would have to wait—I needed the comfort of the carbs!

"It would seem that PC Idle was a wolf in sheep's clothing, if this is to be believed," stated Aunt Loveday.

"It's all lies!" said Mrs. Driscoll. "PC Idle was a proper policeman. He cared about the village—just like his daughter does. He'd be turning in his grave if he knew what's been written about him.

"No smoke without fire," mumbled Aunt Thomasin.

"If it's true, then I doubt he worked alone. There must be other corrupt policemen in the force who are worried about their past coming out."

"An interesting thought Livitha."

I was onto something, I felt sure. "Yes, and maybe that person killed the whistle-blower that the article mentioned."

"It doesn't give a name."

"No, but it could have been one of the women who died recently. Yes!" I exclaimed. "Karyn Montpellier said that Heather Norton was a family friend and had been a good friend of PC Idle's. She died on the moors last week."

"But she was killed by the Beast!"

"She was—supposedly. But what if the killer took the opportunity to kill her so that the Beast would be blamed and so cover up his tracks?"

"Or her, it could be a her," added Aunt Euphemia.

"True, women can be savage, but they do prefer poisoning," Aunt Beatrice said with authority.

"Indeed they do, Beatrice."

The conversation continued. I felt sure that I had uncovered some truth, or at least a useful line of investigation, but the morning was slipping by, and I had to open the shop on time. Taking a final bite of my bread and marmalade followed by a sip of tea, I offered soothing words to Mrs. Driscoll then left for the shop.

Chapter Twenty-Four

Arriving in the village was a shock. If I had thought that Mrs. Driscoll had been exaggerating about the level of fear, I was no longer under any illusions. A large group of villagers had gathered at the centre of the village, a space once used for people to trade and sell their produce. I recognised several familiar faces and customers. Placards raised, they stood in clusters as more people trickled in from the surrounding lanes. As I made a turn, I noticed Karyn Montpellier rise to the centre of the group, loudhailer raised to her mouth. I continued to the shop.

Often, I'd arrive at the shop to be greeted by waiting customers but this morning there was no one standing at the doors, and I guessed I was in for a quiet morning. With plenty of work to do, and another box of freshly made moisturisers and salves to add to the shelves, I was glad of the quiet. However, my aunts had done a good job during my 'training' day and it only took me a few minutes to re-stock the shelves and a few more to sweep the floor until I stood behind the counter increasingly frustrated; outside was where the action was, and it was unlikely that any customers would come in this morning. With that excuse firmly fixed in my mind, I placed a 'Back in five minutes' sign in the window, locked the shop, and made my way to the village centre.

The crowd had grown and was now thick around the central, raised figure of Karyn Montpellier. To my relief, she was talking to the crowd without the use of the loudspeaker, but she was in full flow, her face flushed.

She held up a rolled newspaper, shaking it in the air. "My father was the best of men! It is ridiculous ... ridiculous ... to suggest that he had anything to do with the murders of those women on the moors, but that is what this malicious rag is suggesting!"

Someone from within the crowd booed.

Karyn nodded vociferously. "That's right. It is wrong. He put the killer in prison. He *saved* lives."

"He's a hero!" a voice from the crowd shouted.

"He is a hero!" she agreed. "But this piece," again she shook the paper above her head, "would have you believe that he is not. And do you know why?" She waited, playing her audience.

"No," they replied.

"Because they're trying to cover their mistakes! They let a murderer out of prison and he's back! He's back and he's trying to kill us! This morning he killed Jane Benson. How many more have to die before they admit to their mistake."

A woman sobbed and a young girl close to me tugged at her mother's arm. "I want to go home!"

Mrs. Montpellier was going too far. I understood her outrage, but she was venting her anger and frustration on the crowd and sowing more fear. As I listened, I noticed a police car emerge from a side lane then turn onto the main road out of the village. It was followed by an unmarked police car, and I recognised Garrett at the wheel. He stopped, looked over at the crowd then reversed out of sight.

The mother relented and walked with her daughter away from the crowd. I continued to listen to Karyn's rant. She only stopped to catch breath.

"She's losing it," a man beside me muttered.

"She does seem upset," I replied.

"Aye, but what good's ranting like this going to do? It's the police we need to speak to."

As he spoke, Garrett appeared from the head of the lane and began to walk towards us. Karyn caught sight of him, her flow of words slowing, and then she began to point, stabbing a finger at him. "There he is! That's who is to blame. DCI Garrett Blackwood."

"Not sure how she figures that out. He's not the killer, nor the one who let Leonard Dimmock out of prison."

Undaunted, Garrett walked through the crowd, listened for several moments, then approached Karyn and stood beside her. "May I speak?" For several moments she appeared flustered, but then agreed.

Garrett turned to the crowd. "I know that this is a difficult time," he began, "but I can assure you that we are doing all that we can to apprehend the person who is carrying out these crimes." His tone was guarded, his words carefully chosen.

"How about you put the killer back in prison?" a man shouted. "That'd stop the killings!"

"I'm not at liberty to discuss details. We will be holding a public meeting this evening at seven pm in the village hall where we will present our plan of action and the safety measures we're taking until the situation is resolved. In the meantime, we are increasing the police presence in the village and doubling the task force we have assigned to this case."

"What about Leonard Dimmock? Why can't you put him back in prison?" the man beside me shouted.

Garrett noticed me standing beside the man and seemed to direct his answer at me. "If you come along this evening, we can discuss the issues in further detail. I can explain everything then."

He turned back to Karyn, their words unheard, then stepped down and made his way back through the crowd surrounded by disgruntled mumblings. In a calmer state, Karyn Montpellier continued to talk to the gathered crowd then thanked them for coming and disappeared from sight. The crowd began to disperse and with a grim smile, Garrett made his way over to me.

"Liv."

"Garrett."

"Are you okay?"

I nodded. "Are you? It seems they're out for your blood."

"Comes with the territory. It's a worrying time and when people get scared, they look for scapegoats."

"It's not fair they're blaming you, though."

"I'm a police officer—a fair target. I'm not taking it personally."

"She really was ramping up the fear though."

"So I heard. We'll catch him though, Liv."

I wasn't so sure. Despite the police presence, the killer had only seemed to increase his efforts. "I read that news article."

"Hmm."

"It made an interesting point."

"It did?"

"Yes, it mentioned that the killings were part of a cover up. I wondered if PC Idle had accomplices—someone who could be implicated in his corruption, someone complicit, who could be the killer. Did Heather Norton have information on PC Idle?"

Garrett nodded. "Yes, she was key to the investigation."

"So she was killed to stop her testifying?"

"That's possible."

At that moment Karyn Montpellier strode from what remained of the crowd, her face stony and her eyes set on Garrett.

"DCI Blackwood. I should like a word with you."

"I-"

"It is outrageous that garbage like this is allowed to be printed!" She shook the unfolded newspaper at him.

"Well-"

"My father's name is being dragged through the mud whilst a killer is on the prowl, and we are his prey!"

"Now-"

"Why are you trying to blame my father, DCI Blackwood?" Her face had flushed to puce, her eyes bloodshot, and there were dark circles beneath them. "Why? It is monstrous. Take Dimmock back into prison and all this stops!"

A small crowd had gathered around us. Mr. Montpellier stood beside his wife.

"Mrs. Montpellier. I can assure you that Leonard Dimmock is under surveillance and that he has not been in this vicinity. In fact, he hasn't left the town he was placed in since being released into the community."

"But that can't be!" she spluttered. "The murders started as soon as he was released from prison!"

"It's not him, then!" a woman stated.

"It is! It is him. He's the killer," Karyn Montpellier blurted. "And if you don't arrest him and put him back in prison, I'll ... I'll kill him myself!"

"Karyn!" Mr. Montpellier pressed his hand down on her shoulder.

"Mrs. Montpellier. I suggest that you calm down and go home."

"Don't mind her, DCI Blackwood," Mr. Montpellier said. "She's struggling to come to terms with all of this."

"I understand," replied Garrett."

Mr. Montpellier slipped an arm across her shoulder, "Come along, Karyn. You've had a tough morning. Let's go home and talk about it there. Perhaps DCI Blackwood would be so kind as to continue the conversation in private? You can explain your concerns to him then."

As he spoke, I noticed the scratches on her hands. Rather than being healed, there seemed to be more of them. I noticed too, the drop of blood on her collar. I scanned her. There was also a brown stain on her bootlace and the boots appeared to have been scrubbed.

Surprisingly subdued, perhaps realising how inappropriate her outpouring of venom was, she allowed herself to be led away and Garrett walked with me back to the shop. Once inside, I made us a cup of tea.

"Well, that was interesting!" I said.

"Hah! That's an understatement."

"I can't believe how riled she got although her husband *was* in here last week asking for help. He's at the end of his tether with her moods."

"She certainly showed her true colours this morning," Garrett agreed and took a sip of his tea. "That's a good one, Liv," he said.

"Thanks," I replied. I sipped my own, enjoying the soothing effects of the elixir. It crossed my mind that perhaps I was adding it rather too often but quickly pushed the thoughts away. I needed it right now—particularly with Garrett sat across from me.

"Did you notice the scratches on her hands?"

He nodded. "I did."

"And the blood on her collar and on her shoes."

"On the shoes? No. But the collar, yes."

"Odd."

"Probably from the scratches on her hands. They look like they're getting infected."

"I offered her some balm, but she said she had some antiseptic cream already."

"Doesn't look like she used it."

"I think some of them are fresh."

"They did look fresh. What are you saying, Liv?"

"I don't know. It's just odd that she has scratches like that. She told me they were from gardening."

"It's possible."

"Possible, but odd."

"I concur, DCI Erickson," he laughed.

"Don't you think it's too much of a coincidence that the killings started when Leonard Dimmock was released from prison."

"It's a coincidence, I agree."

"How old is he now?" I asked.

"Seventy-three."

"And the women he's killing-"

"That are being killed."

"Okay, the women that are being killed, they're old too."

Garrett nodded. "Yes, the victims are elderly. The first was over sixty, the two ladies we found the other night were in their eighties, and this morning's victim was in her seventies."

"It's strange that such old women would be out on the moors."

"Well, Heather Norton, was fit and a regular walker on the moors. The two ladies in their eighties were sisters scattering the ashes of one of their husbands who had been an ardent walker in his day. One was in better shape than the other and they were found close to their car so hadn't walked far."

"So, the killer is opportunistic and seeks out the weak."

"I concur with that."

"So, do you think that it means the killer is older. I mean, he's too weak to attack someone younger and stronger?"

"You could be right."

"And if the victims were found close to the road, then that would suggest the killer isn't going deep into the moors. Could he be travelling up here and getting lucky?"

"Not sure I'd call it lucky."

"You know what I mean though. He travels up and kills suitable weak victims who have parked close to where he is. So it could be Leonard Dimmock."

"Given his current location what you suggest is possible, but there's evidence that suggests he wasn't guilty in the first place. That's why he had been let out of prison. There's an on-going investigation of the original investigation. It seems that there may have been a miscarriage of justice."

"Are you saying that Leonard Dimmock was innocent? I thought he was let out on a technicality?"

"It's a little more complex than that, but yes, it does look as though he could be innocent."

"That's awful! He spent decades behind bars."

"It is awful which is why we have to take it so seriously. Add to that that he hasn't left town since his release and that he is already dead, and I'd say it wasn't him," Garrett added dryly.

"Already dead?"

"Yes, he died two days ago—heart attack. He hadn't left his accommodation for days prior to that so we can rule him out as the killer."

"Well, you can't get more ruled out than dead," I said. "Poor man, free only to die."

"Yes, a tragedy if he wasn't the killer."

"Just awful," I agreed. "So it's a copycat situation."

"It certainly *looks* that way."

"Which ties in with my idea of it being someone covering up their tracks—someone involved with the PC Idle crimes!"

"It's an interesting avenue to follow up on," Garrett admitted. "I'll pass the idea on to the team that are managing the investigation."

"You're not?"

"Nope, not my remit this time."

"So, who do you think the killer is and was?"

He gave me the stock answer, "We're working on several lines of enquiry."

I made no mention of Garrett's pregnant ex and with his cup of tea finished, a promise to call me later, and a platonic kiss on my cheek, he left the shop. I made another cup of tea, put an extra drop of elixir in it, then dusted the already clean shelves until the door opened to a gaggle of excited crones.

Chapter Twenty-Five

Having all four aunts in the shop was unusual, to see them so animated even more so. As the door closed behind them, their chatter filled the room.

"Livitha! We have some news."

There was a momentary silence as four pairs of eyes focused on me.

"You have?"

Aunt Beatrice nodded her head vociferously. Aunt Thomasin offered a tentative smile.

"Oh, yes!" said Aunt Euphemia.

"And it involves the Blackwoods," said Aunt Loveday.

"Garrett?"

"And Tobias."

"And the Grimstone Blackwoods."

"I've never heard of them."

"Oh, there's so much that you don't know."

"Well, you can't blame her for not knowing. It's not as if they advertise the fact."

"Indeed."

"Would you?"

"Oh, no."

The conversation was meandering. I brought it back into focus. "So what is it that you know about the Blackwoods?"

"Well-"

"There's a scandal!"

"And a curse!"

"Something very, very suspicious!"

"And it explains everything!"

Whatever it was, sounded bad. "Tell me," I said in exasperation, "how it involves Garrett."

"And Tobias. Don't forget Tobias."

"I have to say, Euphemia, that you seem overly interested in Tobias. I think that you may still carry a torch for him."

"Tsk! I won't deign that comment with a reply."

"Hah! You just did."

"What exactly is it that you've discovered?"

"Livitha, now ... why don't you sit down a moment," suggested Aunt Loveday. "We have some disturbing news."

She was in earnest and so I sat on the stool behind the counter.

"Now ... as you know, we have been away-"

"You disappeared without telling me and left me as a goat stuck in the field with Old Mawde and Hegelina Fekkit all night long!" I said. I hadn't forgiven them for that.

"It's character building, dear, to face ... such challenges."

"Challenges! You turned me into a goat! Garrett saw me ... with udders." My cheeks began to sting at the memory.

"He wouldn't have known it was you, dear."

"But he does!" I countered.

Again, all four aunts stared at me.

"Never mind. Please, tell me what you've discovered."

"Well, we had good reason to leave Haligern and, yes, we should have told you that we were leaving," Aunt Loveday conceded, "although turning you into a goat was necessary."

"We had to be cruel to be kind."

"Indeed."

"You weren't thinking straight."

"She was deranged."

"I was not deranged!"

"She was being ... delinquent!"

"That's a poor choice of word, Beatrice. She had become hysterical and was making poor choices."

"I was upset. Not hysterical," I countered.

"Well, yes, upset then, but you were making poor decisions and we had to stop you."

"Fine. Okay, but please, the next time you think I'm making poor decisions don't turn me into a goat!"

"There are other creatures-"

"No! Just talk to me. Reason with me. How about that?"

Aunt Loveday sighed. "We can talk about the rights and wrongs of our decision another time, dear, but-"

"It's traditional. We were just following tradition."

"Tradition?"

"Yes, the cursing of crones by turning them into goats—it's a Haligern tradition."

"It's certainly becoming one," I grumbled.

"Also, it's coven law," added Aunt Thomasin. "So we were just following the law."

"Oh, Thomasin, I fear you are getting your laws confused. We did what we did to help Livitha in that moment."

"The end justified the means!" stated Aunt Beatrice.

I shook my head. "Well, can we just agree that you're not to help me in that particular way again?"

"Well-"

"You're kidding? You would do it again, wouldn't you?"

"Well-"

"Let us get back to why we're here, sisters."

"Oh, yes, the Blackwood curse!"

"We have discovered that a Blackwood is living on the moors-"

"A cursed Grimstone Blackwood!" interrupted Aunt Beatrice. "In the farmhouse!"

"Yes, in the farmhouse. Thank you, Beatrice."

"Close to where those women were killed!" Aunt Beatrice added, eyes widened and sparkling.

"Is he called Finn?"

All four stared at me in surprise. Aunt Beatrice's look of triumph disappeared.

"You know him?"

"I know that Garrett's cousin is staying in the farmhouse. He's working on an important project and needed somewhere quiet to stay."

"Hah!"

"A likely story!"

"Isn't it true?" I asked.

"Well ... it may be true that he's working on a project, but it's too much of a coincidence that a Blackwood of the Grimstone branch arrives on the moor and then the killings begin," stated Aunt Beatrice in theatrically ominous tones.

"I doubt he's working on a project and more likely that he is hiding out."

"I suspect he's in some sort of witness protection programme," stated Aunt Thomasin. "I'm not sure I believe Millicent's explanation of the situation."

"You mean Garrett and Tobias Blackwood know all about it and are hiding him!"

"Indeed."

"But Millicent doesn't know he's on the moor."

"Indeed, but I'm not sure that's relevant to the situation."

Again, I was lost in the fog of their conversation. "Are you saying that Finn Blackwood is the Beast of Wolfstane Moor?"

"Livitha, the Beast of Wolfstane Moor has become a legend, but it is one based on fact. Over the centuries there have been sightings of werewolves on the moor. The truth is that the Blackwood family have been cursed for generations and no matter how hard they try to hide it there have been slip-ups. The moon is a powerful mistress."

My thoughts travelled to the room at Blackwood Manor with its gouged panelling and shackled chair. "So Garrett *could* be a carrier?"

Aunt Euphemia looked away.

"It's possible, although ... yes, it's possible."

"And so could the child the woman carries."

"Garrett's baby?" I asked.

All four aunts nodded although all avoided making eye contact.

"What evidence do you have that Finn is the Beast of Wolfstane Moor?"

"Well, he carries the curse. We confirmed it at the W. I."

"We went on a research trip," explained Aunt Thomasin. "That's why we weren't at home."

"We discovered that Finn Blackwood is wanted for various, undisclosed, misdemeanours and that he had gone into hiding," added Aunt Loveday. "And then we discovered that he was living at the farmhouse-"

"That was so clever of you, Loveday," said Aunt Euphemia. "It was her that suggested we go up to the moor and see who was living in the house. You recognised him immediately, didn't you, Loveday?"

Aunt Loveday nodded, a smile at the corner of her mouth. "It was so close to where the murders took place, it made sense to take a look."

"The curse must be very strong in him," suggested Aunt Beatrice.

"Why, so, sister?"

"Well, killing the locals isn't the best way to stay undercover, I'd say."

"Foolish indeed!"

"The locals think that the killer is Leonard Dimmock, the man who killed those women in the 1980s. He was released from prison-"

"So Blackwood wouldn't be worried about killing. A released serial killer returning to the scene of the crime to carry out more heinous murders is the perfect cover for a flesh-hunting werewolf."

"You are so clever, Loveday!" Aunt Euphemia exclaimed.

"Thank you, Euphemia," Aunt Loveday said, graciously accepting the compliment.

"Although," I began, "he's definitely not the killer. Garrett confirmed it. After being released from prison he didn't leave the area-."

"He could have used a disguise. Travelled up incognito," suggested Aunt Thomasin.

"And he died several days ago."

"Ah!"

"Well ... are you sure?"

"That's what Garrett told me."

"Another Blackwood!"

"Yes, but that detail demolishes his cousin's cover so perhaps it is true," explained Aunt Thomasin.

"Pity."

Murmurs of agreement.

"But it doesn't mean that Finn Blackwood is not the killer!" exclaimed Aunt Beatrice. "Driven by his lust for flesh and blood the werewolf takes no heed of hiding himself!" she said with a dramatic claw at the air and baring of her teeth.

"I think Beatrice is correct," agreed Aunt Euphemia. "Since when does a werewolf under the influence of the curse care about being caught? They are driven by the urge to attack to the point of insanity!"

I shuddered. My instincts had been right, and Finn had been telling the truth! He'd lied about joking. Did Garrett know the truth? Was he helping to cover up his cousin's murderous activity? Was his loyalty to his cousin greater than his love for me? Obviously. "Finn told me that he'd killed those women! But then said he had been joking!"

"It seems that we were right, sisters," said Aunt Loveday.

"He turned up and the killings began!" I said.

"It's more than a coincidence," added Aunt Euphemia.

"So, is Garrett cursed?" I asked. "Is he a werewolf too?"

Again, all four aunts focused on me; the tension in the room was palpable.

"Have you ever seen him during a full moon?"

"I ... I'm not sure but ... I don't think so."

"Tsk!" Lucifer appeared from the back room and sidled to the steps that led to the main shop and sat surveying us with regal disdain. "Tsk!" he repeated.

Aunt Loveday was the first to respond. "Do you have something to say, Lucifer?"

"Obviously."

In past weeks, Lucifer had become increasingly dismissive and judgemental, his comments bordering on spiteful. He had mentioned grievances and, as he sat there, I was sure he was about to reveal exactly what they were and had no doubt that they involved me.

"It behoves me to speak."

"Does it?" Aunt Thomasin asked with a shake of her head.

He threw her a sideways glance. "It does." He cleared his throat as we waited in silence. "I have to express my surprise that you have not as yet discovered who the real killer is."

"We do know; it's a Blackwood—Finn Blackwood to be precise."

"Pah!" He turned his eyes to me. "I am especially disappointed in you, Livitha. As self-appointed sleuth, have you not yet discovered the truth?"

"Well, I-"

"It was a rhetorical question, Livitha. No you have not."

"I have some ideas-"

"Mostly based on false assumptions and lack of real knowledge."

"Well, I-"

"No! No need to apologise for inadequacies, they are more than apparent."

"I wasn't going to!"

"Now, let me explain, and I will keep it simple in order for you to understand."

Sighs of exasperation followed.

"Finn Blackwood is not the killer," Lucifer stated.

"But he does carry the Blackwood curse and the killings did begin when he arrived, Lucifer," Aunt Loveday explained.

"And he told me that he'd killed the women."

"And retracted that confession, as you yourself have just stated."

"Well-"

"Indeed, believing Finn Blackwood is the killer, or suspecting any Blackwood because they are cursed – circumstantial evidence at best - is exactly the conclusion an inferior mind would come to."

"Lucifer!" I scolded.

"I would mind your Ps and your Qs, Lucifer. Do not forget whose presence you are in."

"As if I ever could!" he spat back.

"Lucifer!" I repeated.

"Lucifer! Lucifer! Lucifer! That is all you ever say to me these days. You are so wrapped up in your own self and wants and needs that you pay no attention to me whatsoever unless it is to chide me." Green eyes settled upon me, wide and challenging.

"Pah! I knew it. He's sulking because Livitha has found someone to love."

"He's jealous!"

"As if that would ever bother me!"

Aunt Loveday shook her head. "Lucifer, could you please explain why you do not believe that Finn Blackwood is the Beast of Wolfstane Moor."

"I did not say that."

"You did!" blurted Aunt Euphemia. "That is exactly what you said."

"No. What I said was that he is not the killer."

"He's trying to blame Garrett Blackwood."

"Or Tobias!" added Aunt Beatrice.

"You do still carry a torch for him!"

"Sisters, please, let us focus on what Lucifer is telling us."

"They continue to insult me, as always. I just shan't bother to explain why you are so very, very wrong in your deductions."

"Hah! Listen to Sherlock Holmes!"

"Thomasin, that's not helping."

"Well, he thinks he is so superior to us!"

"I am."

Aunt Loveday sighed. "Lucifer, please, explain your theory. Sisters, please do Lucifer the honour of listening patiently."

Sighs and huffs.

"Let me put you out of your misery, or rather mine. The victims were mauled, were they not?"

"Yes," I replied. "Mrs. Driscoll said they were shredded."

"But they were not eaten?"

"Eaten!"

"Not that we know of."

"They were not."

"What difference does that make?"

"I know," said Aunt Beatrice. "He's right, you know."

"Then let him explain Beatrice, dear."

"The newest victims, like the ones when you were a teenager, Livitha, were slashed—hunted, yes, but not eaten, so it stands to reason that a Blackwood did not kill them."

"Ah!" Aunt Thomasin nodded in understanding.

"Of course," said Aunt Euphemia.

"Yes, I see," admitted Aunt Loveday.

"That is gross!" My stomach churned with the implication. Lucifer wasn't denying that the Blackwoods weren't killers, just that they weren't guilty of the current spate of murders. The revelation that the true Beast of Wolfstane Moor was a maneater was not something I had fully taken on board. The movies I'd watched as a teenager glossed over that part of werewolf lore. "The Blackwoods eat people!" I whispered.

"Only at the full moon," Lucifer chuckled. "It's not very romantic despite what you watch on the television." He cast me a sly glance, watching me carefully as he spoke. "It's more Hannibal Lecter than Benicio del Toro!"

"Then," said Aunt Loveday, "the killer is a common and garden psychopath.

"Is there anything common and garden about a sociopathic serial killer, dear sister?"

"I mean to say, that they are not of the cursed variety."

"At least not of the lycanthropic kind."

"I do believe that we are looking for a human killer."

"So, not one of our own."

"Indeed."

"Such a relief."

"Indeed."

For my aunts, the drama appeared to be over, and they disappeared as quickly as they had arrived after reminding me to lock the shop before I left. Lucifer's theory as to why the killer wasn't one of the Blackwood clan was sound, and a relief, but the killer was still out there and with the latest victim being killed on the outskirts of the village, becoming increasingly bold.

In between customers, as the winter sun lowered in the sky and with the white-haired fairy bothering me for jobs, I mulled over the evidence. One thing stuck in my mind: the killer was targeting elderly women, unlike the killer who had stalked the moors during my teenage years who had murdered younger women. To me, there were three explanations for this behaviour: a) the killer had a fetish for killing older women, b) the killer was weak/older himself so targeted victims who were easier to kill or c) the killer was a woman. I wasn't familiar with criminal psychology and knew very little about the mind of a serial killer, but these deductions made sense to me.

I felt that the puzzle was beginning to slot into place and there were several other clues that gave me my eureka! moment.

"I know!" I blurted. "I know who did it!"

The fairy chittered with irritation, swooped low, then headed for the grandfather clock.

"Mrs. Montpellier! It was so obvious now. The scratches, the blood, the werewolf costume! She even has a motive."

With five minutes to closing time, I waited impatiently as the clock ticked them away and I could finally turn the sign to 'Closed', lock the door and call Garrett to let him know who I thought the killer was and why, sure that he would agree and set the investigation in motion.

The grandfather clock struck five and I dialled Garrett's number as I flipped the sign. His mobile went straight to answerphone. I left a message then, with frustration mounting, decided to pay Mrs. Karyn Montpellier a visit. She was a talker, had been keen to talk to me when I delivered the giftbox, so I would attempt to glean incriminating evidence from her. I set off for her house with determination, but as I stepped out into the darkness of evening, I noticed the fullness of the moon—the Hunter's moon!

Chapter Twenty-Six

For several moments, I stood transfixed, and the sense of fore-boding that had dogged me over the past days, and particularly since the visit from the gypsy-witch, became overwhelming.

The Hunter's moon!

A full moon!

The celestial call to the cursed.

The dog-whistle of the lycanthrope!

If there were werewolves on the moors, then tonight could be when they revealed themselves. I realised then that there was another reason Lucifer was correct about the Blackwoods. The killer had struck during the period when the moon was a wan-ing crescent and waxing gibbous—not the full moon when the lycanthropic curse could overwhelm its victims.

I shivered as the cold night air brushed my cheek. If I went to his house, would I find Garrett strapped to the chair in the turret room tonight? Should I go to Blackwood Manor and check? Was it him that had carried me to the house the night the evil imp had attacked me in the woods? Had it been Gar-rett transmogrified into a dark-haired werewolf that had held me tight to his musclebound chest? Cradled in that beast's arms I had felt safe, but how could that be if he were a man-eat-ing monster?

A howl broke through my thoughts, and I came to full con-sciousness with a start, heart beating hard.

The howl repeated.

A dog's howl. Not a wolf nor a man-eating werewolf. With a huge sigh of relief, berating myself for being overly dramatic and winding myself into a state of fear, I checked that I had locked the shop door and made my way to Karyn's house.

Light shone from the glass at the side of the front door although the rest of the house appeared to be in darkness suggesting that the hallway light had been left on and Mr. and Mrs. Montpellier were out. Mr. Montpellier had asked Garrett if they could discuss his wife's concerns in private, so it was possible they had arranged a meeting. A wave of concern passed through me, given what I suspected Karyn Montpellier capable of, but I doubted she would try to harm Garrett—at least not in public. As he was a strong man, and not a feeble and elderly woman, he wasn't in any real danger either. Although - proven by the photographs in the hallway - she was handy with a firearm. But ... wouldn't she need a silver bullet? My thoughts jumped from scenario to scenario and, with concern for Garrett bubbling beneath a thin veneer of calm, I gave the house and surrounding area a final scan for people and cameras, then opened the gate. A narrow path led to the back of the house.

It was snooping, illegal even, but as I suspected that she was the murderer, driven to kill in order to save her father's good name, the end justified the means.

There were several clues that led me to believe that Mrs. Montpellier was the murderer. She was a fell runner, quick and agile on her feet even over rocky ground, and she was fast; I'd seen the photographs of her receiving prizes and even seen her running long distance without any evidence of strain. I now believed that it had been her, dressed in the werewolf costume, who had terrorised me on the moors. If she wore the costume when she killed her victims, then it could hold vital and incriminating evidence. Like her collar and shoe, it was perhaps

stained with the blood of her victims; I had to find it. Blood
on the costume would be all the evidence the police needed to
charge her with murder.

Apart from a spate of bloody murders, the village was generally safe, so I was unsurprised when I found the backdoor unlocked. Light from the moon, still low in the sky, gave enough
light to push back the shadows in the kitchen but not enough
to see the level of detail I needed. I raised a flattened palm,
whispered "glæm gebierhtan" and watched as a speck of light
grew to a bright globe of light. It hovered above my palm, illuminating the kitchen around me—too bright. "Dimmian," I
whispered. The light dimmed to a soft glow, just enough to
light my way. Taking several moments to listen and assure myself I was alone in the house, I began my search for the costume.
With no visible sign of the washing machine, I searched behind
each cupboard door to check for integral appliances without
success.

There were two doors leading off from the kitchen, one
led to the utility room, the other gave access to the rest of the
house. There was no sign of the costume in the utility room
either. I deduced that, given that the latest murder had taken
place last night the costume could still be in the washing basket. A risky strategy as far as I was concerned, I'd have burned
the costume rather than risk bringing it home. However, I
wasn't a killer and surely if you were a killer, you wouldn't think
logically either, or perhaps she was so confident in not being
found out that desperately washing away the evidence of her
crime wasn't at the top of her 'To Do' list?

I made my way through to the living room and then up
the stairs to the washing basket but as I took the final riser

and stepped onto the landing where a large wicker basket sat with the lid askew and a tantalisingly furry fabric poked out through the gap, the front door opened, and the hallway filled with voices—Mr. and Mrs. Montpellier had arrived home.

"You really do get yourself into some scrapes, Mistress Erickson." Lucifer's voice was directly behind me, and I swung, witch-light dimming to off, to see him perched on the banister. Eyes of silver, caught in the dimming light, stared at me.

"Lucifer!" I whispered.

The voices downstairs stopped.

"Did you hear that?" Mr. Montpellier asked.

"Hear what?"

"That noise—from upstairs?"

"No!"

Silence.

"See! There's nothing."

Heels tapped in the hallway as Mrs. Montpellier walked into the kitchen. Noise in the hallway faded and then the couple continued their conversation in the kitchen.

"What are you doing here?" I whispered as Lucifer continued to stare at me from his perched position.

"Helping. What else? But this time if you change me into a mouse, I shall not forgive you."

"I don't need help," I hissed.

"Livitha, you have just been caught breaking and entering. That is a crime. You could go to prison."

"Don't exaggerate, Lou, and anyway, I'm onto something. I think Mrs. Montpellier is the Beast of Wolfstane Moor."

Lucifer snorted in derision.

"I have evidence!"

"Circumstantial at best. A few scratches and a blood stain or two do not equate to guilt."

"She has motive! And I bet if those blood stains were analysed, they'd corroborate my supposition."

"Jargon! Speak English, woman! I imagine they would show that she had bled onto her clothes from those scratches."

"And just where did she get the scratches from? Hmm?"

"Her garden," he said dryly. "She has roses, and they have enormous thorns. I know, I've just been stabbed by one. It was like a dagger piercing my skin!"

"What were you doing in the roses?"

"I'd rather not say."

"Right."

"A familiar has to do what a familiar has to do."

"Fine."

"I was taken short. I think the salmon you gave me this morning was off."

"It wasn't!"

"If you'd like to see the evidence, it is in the rose garden."

"Lou, this is not the time or the place for this ... discussion."

"Don't you care that I've suffered?"

"Of course I do, but-"

"Good. It was awful, Livitha. You should never give a cat rotten fish."

"I didn't!"

"It caused ... how shall I put it? An explosive event."

"Ugh! Enough detail."

"Really? I thought you liked detail, Livitha."

"Not that kind, Lucifer! Anyway, listen, there's more evidence. She has a werewolf costume. It was on the line outside.

I think she wears it when she kills. I saw a werewolf on the moors, and I think it was her. She's a fell runner."

"Ah, well if she's a fell runner then she must be guilty," he said with a sardonic tone.

"It means she knows her way around the moors and she's quick—I've seen her run. She's won prizes. And, if she did wear the costume when she killed those women, the evidence could be in its fibres—even if she has washed it."

"An interesting observation, but where is this werewolf costume?"

"That's why I'm up here; I'm looking for it!" I hissed.

Downstairs the conversation had become heated, and Lucifer shushed me as I began to explain about my mission to find the costume. "Listen to them, Livitha, you may discover something important," he said.

Mrs. Montpellier's voice had risen an octave and she now sounded on the verge of hysteria. Her husband's placatory words went unheeded.

"This is all Blackwood's fault!"

"Now, now, dear-"

"Did you hear what he said? Did you?"

"Of course, I was in the room!"

"Well, then you know this is all a ruse to shut me up, but I'll get him."

"Karyn! If you continue talking like that-"

"I have every right to be angry."

"Yes, but you've already threatened him in public."

"And I'll do it again."

"Darling, I know that you're upset, but this is getting out of hand."

"Out of hand! I'll show you out of hand. I'm going to deal with him once and for all."

"It's late. I'm sure he's gone home by now. Call him tomorrow. We can arrange a follow up meeting."

"And say what? What will convince him to stop the investigation? Huh? What?"

"He explained that he's not in charge of the investigation."

"Hah! A likely story. He's just fobbing me off."

"Let's open a bottle of wine and talk it over."

A short silence was followed by a murmur of acceptance and then the clink of glasses. As the drinks were poured, I checked the washing basket but was disappointed to discover that the furry fabric was a cushion cover.

"It's not here," I said.

"That's because it's here." Lucifer stood in a bedroom doorway and disappeared back into the room with a superior flick of his tail as I turned to him.

With light steps as the conversation downstairs resumed, I followed Lucifer to an open wardrobe.

"Shine your light in there," he commanded.

Witch light reactivated, the werewolf costume's mangey fur came into view, the masked hood sitting at a twisted angle forming a grotesque face.

"Check it for blood, then."

"Give me a chance!"

"We don't have much time," he urged. "We could be discovered at any moment."

"We will if you don't stop talking," I whispered.

I shone the light into the wardrobe and checked the fabric for signs of blood. None was apparent.

"It's clean."

"No, Livitha, it is not. I can smell the blood. Check it."

I took hold of an arm and raised it to my nose. "It smells freshly laundered to me," I said.

"Such inferior olfactory senses! Check again."

"Perhaps you're wrong?"

Lucifer snorted.

Once more I shone the witch-light at the fabric. Again there was nothing to see. I ran my hand along the front and noticed a patch where the fabric felt different. When I pulled my hand back it was smeared with blood.

"It's blood!"

"It is, and it's fresh, and now it's on you."

"Why would you put a bloodied costume back in the wardrobe?"

"I didn't."

"The murderer, Lou. Why would the murderer put a bloodied costume back in the cupboard? It's incriminating evidence."

"No idea."

The argument downstairs moved into the hallway and, unwilling to step into the wardrobe with the bloodied costume, I slipped through the open door of another bedroom, only just concealing myself as Mrs. Montpellier's head appeared as she came up the stairs. Mr. Montpellier followed as she ranted about how she was going to deal with Garrett once and for all whilst he tried to talk her out of a confrontation that could 'ruin her career'.

With neither side conceding, silence fell between them. I waited as they moved around their bedroom. Minutes turned into half an hour as Mrs. Montpellier went back and forth among the rooms, going downstairs then returning upstairs whilst Mr. Montpellier watched the television in the bedroom. With them both moving about the house there was no opportunity for me to leave. I considered climbing through the window but quickly changed my mind. I listened as Neil Montpellier left his bedroom, padded across the landing, and went into the bathroom. Mrs. Montpellier also left their bedroom.

"Where are you going?" Mr. Montpellier shouted as she ran down the stairs.

"Up to that farmhouse. It's where he goes every night."

"How do you know that?"

"I know."

"Karyn! Have you been following him?"

"What if I have."

Mr. Montpellier sighed. "Not again, Karyn!"

"It's not the same."

"If they ... Listen to me, Karyn. You can't go up there. You'll end up with another restraining order."

"Hah! They can try."

"Your dad's not here to help this time. You'll ruin your political career! Think of the business!"

"What does that matter if my father's name is destroyed?" she shouted back now on the landing. Footsteps followed as she ran down the stairs and then left the house.

Minutes passed, the toilet flushed, and Mr. Montpellier returned to his bedroom. Itching to leave and warn Garrett that the woman was on her way I was about to open the door when Mr. Montpellier stepped onto the landing, ran down the stairs, and followed his wife out of the house. With them both gone, I returned to their bedroom to take a photograph of the incriminating evidence but when I opened the door to the wardrobe, the costume had gone.

"She's going to kill him, Lou! She's going onto the moors to kill Garrett!"

Chapter Twenty-Seven

It was only when I stepped out of the kitchen door into the garden that I remembered I didn't have a car, indeed, I no longer owned a functioning car, mine being a heap of smouldering metal.

Panic set in.

"How am I supposed to get to the moors now? She's way ahead of me!"

"Liv."

Oblivious to Lucifer calling my name I dialled Garrett's number. "Come on! Pick up!" An automated voice answered, requesting that I leave a message after the beep. "Garrett, it's Liv. Call me as soon as you get this message. It's urgent … Karyn Montpellier … she's angry and threatening to hurt you! She's trying to track you down."

Frustrated, I marched down the path, unsure of my next move. I had to get to the moor.

"Liv!"

"What is it, Lucifer? I've got to get to Garrett. What am I going to do? I don't have a car!"

Lucifer sighed. "Liv." He flicked his tail. "Follow me." He disappeared behind the house, tail high.

"Oh, what is it? I really can't play games now. I've got to get to the farmhouse!"

"Come and look," he called.

Lucifer stood at the back of the house where a number of gardening tools were propped against a wheelbarrow filled with the thorny debris from a session of rose pruning.

"Liv."

"What is it, Lucifer? I can't read your mind."

"Or see what's in front of your very eyes!"

"There's a wheelbarrow with a rake and a spade propped against it," I said dryly.

"Choose one."

"For what? Oh, you can't be serious."

"Why not?" he said. "You've ridden on a plastic broom, why not a spade, or a rake. How about using the wheelbarrow?"

"Is that a joke?"

"No."

"Well, it should be. I am not hurtling through the air in a wheelbarrow!"

"But it will be comfortable."

"For whom?"

"Me."

I sighed. There was no way I was going to use the wheelbarrow – it was just too ridiculous – but the rake, with its longer handle, was a contender. "Oh, I can't though. What if Millicent finds out? She's already pencilled me into her bad books. She thinks I'm bringing the coven into disrepute. She could have me sent to the Academy!" Millicent's disapproving words rose in my mind, 'We must live among humans without notoriety, sisters, without disrepute. We all know what happens when humans begin to fear us.'

"Bringing?"

"Yes, Lou, bringing."

"Brought is the correct tense, Livitha."

"I haven't got time for this!"

"Well, choose!"

"But we're supposed to live among humans without noto-riety!"

"Too late. I have been around witches for centuries, Livitha. Believe me when I tell you that your kind is continu-ally bringing disrepute down upon themselves and you are all, in the main, notorious for some thing or the other. Why do you think there are so many stories and moving pictures about you?"

"But ... Millicent."

"You must not fear Millicent, Livitha. Therein lies a path-way to great darkness," he stated. His green eyes flashed, and his tail whipped from side to side. "However, now is not the time for that conversation. Choose your mode of transport and be quick; time is not on our side. I favour the barrow."

I dismissed the barrow then eyed the other tools. "I'll look ridiculous—again."

"So it's something you're familiar with—good."

"I choose ... the rake. The spade is too short."

"Good choice."

Without further hesitation I took hold of the rake. Strad-dling the handle, and with Lucifer on my shoulder, I began to focus on rising. Unstable, adrenaline already pumping through my veins, we rose above the kitchen window and then with a jolt of power accelerated, hurtling across the lawn on an up-ward trajectory only just missing a cluster of shrubs. Cold wind bit at my cheeks and whipped through my hair as my feet brushed against branches. We continued to rise, hurtling to-wards the Hunter's moon, a polished silver disc against the dark sky.

Although it was dark, I was cautious about being seen and rose higher, way above the rooftops and tallest trees. It was surprisingly, bitingly, cold. Lucifer, at my shoulder, pressed against my head. With my fingers already becoming numb, we left the village behind and headed out onto the moors.

"Faster, Livitha," Lucifer shouted into my ear. "Faster!"

I focused ahead, dug deep into my core, and we shot forward.

Lucifer's talons sunk into my shoulder as he was thrust backwards. "Yeehaa!" he cried.

He was enjoying the ride and, despite the cold, so was I. Flying was thrilling and I focused on gradually increasing our speed. The one downside to putting my foot down was that it burnt through my energy, and it only took minutes before I felt the first sensations of fatigue. I slowed, relieved to see the rising hills of the moor ahead and then the single yellow light shining from the farmhouse window.

As we approached the house, I swooped low in an effort to remain unseen, and came to a running, hopping stop. Lucifer yowled his annoyance and jumped from my shoulder, taking the opportunity for a spiteful spiking of claws. "I won't be giving you port any time soon," I grumbled once I'd managed to regain my balance and untangle my feet from the rake's metal head.

"I heard that. Another strike against you, Livitha. I have a list of all the intolerable situations I'm having to deal with whilst being your familiar."

"Whatever your grievances are, Lucifer, and I really cannot understand why you're being so mean, they will have to wait," I said, my patience worn thin by his unreasonable attitude.

"I shall bring it before the Council."

"Fine. You can complain as much as you like afterwards."

"I will."

"Good."

With rancour between us, I gripped the rake and made my way to the house. Light shone from the downstairs windows illuminating the front yard. A car that I didn't recognise was parked in front of the house and, in the distance, an engine, pushed to its limits, roared.

Now was not a time to be shy so I leant my rake up against the yard wall and scrambled over. Thankfully, the rocks were stable and the wall not too high. After jumping down to the other side I strode with purpose to save the man I loved from a maniacal killer (even if he was one himself) and knocked on the door.

The engine in the distance had grown close; she was coming!

The door swung open to reveal Garrett. Behind him, a glass in hand, the fire roaring in the hearth, sat a very chilled Finn relaxing on the sofa. Questioning frowns were quickly replaced by smiles.

"Liv."

"Garrett, I-"

"Come in, Liv."

"I didn't hear you drive up. Come in."

"She didn't drive," Lucifer stated.

"You've brought your cat?" Garrett asked with a bemused smile.

"I'm her familiar, you dunce."

"It's her familiar, Gar, be careful what you say, they can be beasts," advised Finn.

"Hah! Fine words coming from you!" Lucifer flicked his tail and strode into the house, heading for the fireplace.

"Make yourself at home, why don't you," Finn quipped.

Lucifer sat before the fire in regal disdain, his favourite stance of late. "I will, thanks."

Neither Finn nor Garrett reacted to Lucifer's meowed responses.

The noise of cars hurtling through the narrow and winding moorland lanes grew muffled as Garrett closed the door.

"What is it, Liv? You seem flustered. Did you walk?"

"She flew, idiot!" meowed Lucifer.

"Lou! That's enough," I scolded. "Ignore him," I said. "He's been in a bad mood lately."

"Finn took a sip of his drink and contemplated Lucifer. "Can't understand a word you say, I'm afraid," he said then turned to me. "He can be as rude as he likes, we won't understand."

"I can make myself understood!" Lucifer meowed. "I choose not to."

"What's wrong, Liv?" asked Garrett. "Come in and have a drink."

"Didn't you get my message?" I stepped inside. "I left a message."

"No. There's no signal up here. Was it important?"

"It's a nuisance!" said Finn. "There are people I really need to see!"

"Patience, Finn, I'm working on it."

Finn downed the rest of his drink and began to pour another. A small frown from Garrett hinted at his disapproval but he said nothing.

"Liv?"

"Yes! It was important. I know who the killer is and she's coming here to kill you!"

"She?" Garrett's frown deepened. "Who is she and why would she be coming to kill me?"

"Looks like Liv is quite the sleuth. Who is it, Liv? Who is it that wants to kill our valiant policeman?"

"It's Karyn Montpellier. She's in a rage about the investigation into her father."

Garrett groaned. "I met with her earlier. She did seem upset. But there really is nothing I can do. I'm not in charge of the investigation. I explained to her that there's a special unit involved."

"Then why does she blame you?"

"Because ... the first victim, Mrs. Heather Norton, she came to me with her concerns and PC Idle's deathbed confession."

"Now this sounds juicy!" Finn said.

Chapter Twenty-Eight

"Deathbed confession?"

"Yes, PC Idle admitted that he'd tampered with the evidence in the original Beast of Wolfstane Moor case. Basically, he'd framed Leonard Dimmock."

"So, he *was* innocent."

"Tampering with evidence isn't enough to claim his innocence. It does mean that the case against him was null and void though. But what really bothered Mrs. Norton was that she came to believe that PC Idle was the real killer and he had framed Leonard Dimmock to cover up his own guilt. He was rambling towards the end; hallucinating – or so she thought. Talked about killing those women; how he'd done it, what he'd worn, the trophies he'd saved."

"Did he dress up as a werewolf to kill?" I asked.

"So he said in his ramblings, but given his state, it's hard to say what's real and what's not. How did you know?"

"I've seen the costume! There are photographs of him in it from years ago and ... I found it in their wardrobe. It had fresh blood on it. Mrs. Montpellier is the killer, Garrett, and she's coming here to kill you."

"You really must have upset her, Gar," Finn said dryly.

"This is serious," I snapped. "She's a killer!"

"Yes, of old ladies, not of Blackwoods." Finn seemed unperturbed by my revelations. "Have a glass of whisky, Liv. It'll help with the nerves," he held up the bottle.

"I'm fine!" I replied a little more sharply than was polite, irked by his nonchalance. "This is serious. Garrett, she's on her way!"

"Liv, Finn is right. So far, if she is the killer, she has only killed elderly women. I'm sure we can deal with her—if she turns up."

As he spoke headlights beamed in through the windows and tyres came to a hard stop.

"Speak of the devil!"

"And he shall appear. Or she in this instance." Garrett turned to the door.

"Garrett! Wait!"

"Liv, it's fine. I can handle this."

"I know, but-"

"I'll go, Gar. I'll tell her your not here. How about that?" Finn rose from his seat.

"No! It might not be her. You're supposed to be-" Garrett glanced from Finn to me, "keeping a low profile." He turned to me. "I'll explain about Finn later, Liv. There's lots to talk about. I've kept you in the dark, and I'm sorry, but it had to be done."

"About why Finn is here?"

Garrett nodded. "And some other ... things." He turned to the door and opened it. Car headlights flooded the room.

The next moments were a blur.

Garrett stepped out into the yard to the slamming of a car door. Finn moved from the sofa to the door as I followed Garrett. The headlights were blinding, and it wasn't until we stood directly before them that the figure of Karyn Montpellier could be seen. After listening to her rising hysteria back at the house, I had expected her to be argumentative, perhaps even shouting at Garrett. In my mind's eye, she had also been wearing the werewolf costume. Instead, she stood in her ordinary clothes, face deadpan, a gun raised and pointed at Finn.

"I told you to stop the investigation, Blackwood!" she called. "You've destroyed my father's name."

Before Garrett had a chance to react, a snarling werewolf, rubbery fangs hanging in an open mouth, hurtled from the shadows, a large knife held aloft in its huge and hairy fist. Mrs. Montpellier screamed, the gun fired, and the werewolf launched itself with a bounding step. The knife glinted in the moonlight.

Wounded, Finn staggered against the door at the exact moment the knife arced down over Garrett and Lucifer jumped onto the werewolf's head. Blinded Lou's furry belly, the werewolf missed Garrett's chest and instead cut through the sleeve of his jacket. It roared as Lucifer's claws sunk deep into its scalp.

Mrs. Montpellier stood transfixed by Finn's struggles to stand but then became aware of Garrett. Momentarily confused, and realising her mistake, she quickly swung her gun to point in his direction.

With Finn staggering back inside the house, the werewolf wrestling with the cat pinned to its head, and Garrett about to be shot, I took aim. A powerful surge of energy rose from my core, travelled to my shoulders, and burst out through each of my fingers. Thin rods of charged and sparking energy shot at Mrs. Montpellier like bolts of lightning. The pain in my fingertips was intense. The stone wall that formed the yard's boundary sparked as the bolts hit, illuminating dark and hooded figure as though caught in the flash of a camera, and Mrs. Montpellier's gun flew out of her hands, landing with a crack against the stone wall. She was thrown against the car and landed with a thud.

I turned my attention to the werewolf. It was circling wildly, batting at Lucifer as he yowled in pain, still pinned to the head, claws sunk deep.

Too afraid of hurting Lucifer, I couldn't use the energy in my hands against the werewolf, but as I sought wildly in my mind for another spell to use, the werewolf screamed in pain, dropped his knife, and began pulling at the mask in a desperate effort to remove the cat.

I took the opportunity to retrieve the knife and threw it across the yard into the shadows.

Lucifer jumped from the werewolf's head, landing beside me.

Bind him. Tie him with your magick. 'Gebind him. Becnyttan him mid drylic'

"Yes. A binding spell!"

"Quickly, Liv!" Lucifer urged.

From the depths of my knowledge, I drew on the ancient voices and, as words formed, I began to chant, focusing on the ivy that grew up the front of the house. Vines slithered across the yard, one long tendril joined by others, diverging to streak across the ground. Mrs. Montpellier screamed. The werewolf tugged the mask back into place, unaware of the approaching vegetation.

Within seconds the vine was winding around their feet, then their legs, up their torsos, and wrapping their arms against their sides until they were firmly bound and gagged.

Stop! "Gestillaþ!"

Lucifer pressed himself against my ankle. "Finally, you've done something useful," he snipped.

Heart beating hard, I laughed in relief. "Yes! I've done it."

"About time," he said.

"Oh, Lou!" He winced as I picked him up but didn't resist and I cradled him in my arms. "You saved Garrett," I said. "You were very, very brave. Are you hurt?"

He began to purr as I stroked his head. "Just a flesh wound."

As he spoke, I remembered the figure that had been illuminated by my blasts of magical energy and then the falling figure of Finn.

I turned, Lucifer in my arms, to see Garrett disappearing back into the house and behind him, the cloaked figure followed. A wisp of blonde hair protruded from the hood. His girlfriend!

With a final glance at the bound figures, and ignoring their shouts, I followed the woman and Garrett into the house. Finn was crouched beside the hearth and the woman ran to kneel beside him. As he buckled and collapsed, the injury became obvious; a large and blooming patch of blood seeped through the wool of his Arran knit jumper.

"He's been shot!" I gasped. "I'll call an ambulance."

"No!" Garrett's hand gripped my arm. "We can deal with this."

"But Garrett, he could die without the right treatment. He's been shot."

"Jofrid will care for him."

"Your girlfriend?" I pulled my arm from his grip.

"She's not my girlfriend, Liv."

"She's carrying your baby, what else would you call her?"

"She's not carrying my baby."

"But ..." I glanced over at the woman now cradling Finn's head on her knees, her swollen belly touching his hair. It was obvious that she cared deeply for him. It was also obvious that she wasn't distraught at his injury. A thought began to form. "He was shot."

"That's right."

"But he's not dying."

"He's not."

"Because it wasn't a silver bullet."

"Correct."

"She's good, Gar." Finn's voice was pained.

"Shh! Don't talk. Rest, my love," Jofrid soothed.

"The baby is Finn's," I declared.

"Yes, it is."

"It's not yours," I stated, relief surging.

"No, it's not."

Tears welled and in a moment of spontaneous and absolute relief, I flung my arms around him, all anger, resentment, and despair gone. He held me firm against his chest. "I'm sorry, Liv. I'm sorry that I couldn't tell you."

I could only nod into his chest, desperately holding back the tears, the fizzing in my fingers, and the whirling vortex of emotion at my core—now was not the time to spontaneously combust with wayward magick!

"The prophesy," I said, easing myself from Garrett's arms. "The prophecy came true."

"What prophecy?"

Chapter Twenty-Nine

"A gypsy came into the shop and demanded I cross her palm with silver. She said that the beast would fall on the moor and blood would be on the hearth! If Finn is the ... well, a ... I'm not sure how to say it-"

"A werewolf?" Garrett suggested.

"Yes, a werewolf."

"The Beast of Wolfstane Moor?"

"Is he?"

"It's a legend, but has its roots among the Blackwoods, yes."

"Then, he is the Beast that fell, and he did bleed on the hearth," I said. "But the rest of the prophecy hasn't happened."

"Why, what else did she say?"

"I remember it clearly now,

Upon the moor his heart will beat.

Upon the hearth his blood will seep.

The Beast will fall, and you will weep.

The Blackwood Curse is yours to keep."

"I guess you could say it has come true."

"Yes, but the 'Blackwood Curse is yours to keep'? What does that mean?"

"I don't know. Perhaps she was playing you, Liv."

"No! I really don't think so."

Garrett turned his attention to Finn as he groaned. Jofrid continued to stroke his forehead with soothing fingers. "Can we get him to a bed?" she asked.

The next minutes were spent making Finn comfortable. He refused to go to bed and instead sat on the sofa with another dram of whiskey and the knitted blanket that Jofrid insisted on wrapping round him, over his knees. "Nothing keeps a Blackwood down, at least not for long," he smiled then downed the whiskey. "I thought you were supposed to be keeping me safe, Gar," he joked.

"I will," replied Garrett, "at least from those that can really harm you."

Finn nodded, then closed his eyes and leant back into the sofa.

"What's going on, Garrett?" I asked. "What's all of this about?"

"Give me a minute. I have to call this in and then I'll tell you everything."

Whilst Garrett contacted Police HQ to report the attack, I made coffee for us in the kitchen. As I poured milk into a mug, he joined me.

"It's a long and complicated story, Liv, and I'll tell you the basics, but first, give me a kiss. The past few days have been hell without you."

His arm slipped around my waist and for once I didn't care that he could feel how overly plump my middle was and turned to kiss his waiting lips. All the badness of the world melted away as we held each other, and he released me with a sigh.

"Now," he said, once more DCI Blackwood, "this information is between us—you're not to tell your aunts, or anyone else. Do you understand?"

"Yes, sir!" I joked in response to his officious tone and offered him a mug of steaming coffee.

"Thanks. So, Finn is here under my protection. He's been working to uncover corruption. For years there have been rumours, dark stories ... so dark." Garrett looked beyond my shoulder.

"Go on."

"I will, but the horrors he has uncovered, Liv ..."

"But who? Billionaires? Politicians? Is it an Epstein situation?"

He shook his head. "It's not among the humans, Liv."

"Not among the humans? Then where?"

"At the Academy."

"The Academy for Advanced Witchcraft?"

He nodded. "Yes. Finn has evidence that the Academy has been infiltrated by witches that have turned to the dark side. They've hidden themselves well and manipulated the covens for decades. We've been concerned for a number of years, but they're masters at covering their tracks."

"Someone must have known! Why didn't they speak out?"

"They corrupt people, Liv, corrupt them so that they're too afraid to speak out and have their dirty secrets revealed. Finn is here because we think they're onto him and with Jofrid carrying his child, mother and baby could become targets too. It would be a classic move to use them against him."

It was beginning to make sense. "You said it was dark ..."

"Finn was investigating the disappearance of several children. The trail led him back to the Academy."

"No!"

He nodded. "I'm afraid so."

"But why would they take children?"

"To traffic them. Take them to the other realms where they're traded. Dark magick hexes often use ... body parts."

"That's ... horrifying!"

"It is and given who he suspects is involved, he's in grave danger."

I glanced at Jofrid, so heavily pregnant. "And so is his baby," I said with a shiver of apprehension.

"It is. Exactly. His greatest joy has become his greatest weakness," Garrett said with sadness.

"We can help them, though! Me, my aunts-"

"No! You mustn't tell them."

"But they know he's here," I said taken aback by the ferocity of his response. "You don't think they're involved do you?"

"No! Not at all. It's just that the fewer people who know ..." He glanced over to the hearth. "We'll have to find a different safehouse; this one is compromised." He sighed. "Your aunts are good women, I trust them, but we really can't let anyone know that Finn and Jofrid are here. If word leaked out ..."

"I understand."

"The trafficking has been going on for centuries," Finn added. "But we're going to put a stop to it, aren't we, Gar."

"That's right," Garrett agreed.

"Shh, my love. Let your body heal," soothed Jofrid.

"It's just awful!"

"Yes, it is. Dark magick ultimately corrupts, which is why it is forbidden."

"When witches go bad, they go *bad*!" Finn stated.

The distant wail of police sirens growing loud brought the attackers back to our attention and we returned to the yard where Karyn Montpellier and the werewolf lay bound.

"I can understand why Karyn would want to kill you-"

"Thanks!"

"You know what I mean. She has grievances. She's churned up about her father-" The bound woman began to squirm, straining against the vines and shouting through the one held like a horse's bit in her mouth. "I think I know who this is." I pointed to the faux werewolf. "But why would *he* be killing women on the moors dressed as a werewolf?"

Garrett stood over the wriggling creature and tugged at the mask. It slipped off as he yanked it to reveal Neil Montpellier.

"As I suspected," I said.

"It was obvious." Lucifer was once again by my side, slinking between my ankles. "I knew from the start that it was him."

"Oh, Lou! You did not."

"I did!"

"Okay, so explain why he killed all of those women."

"It's simple; he loves his wife."

"He loves his wife so kills other women."

"More likely he hated his wife so killed other women—or his mother," suggested Garrett.

"Poppycock!" replied Lucifer with disdain. "Flaccid pseudo-Freudian pop-psychology."

I know how we can find out, I said, remembering one of the spells Aunt Thomasin had gifted me. "I'll make him tell us the truth."

"Make it quick, Livitha," Lucifer demanded. "Not only am I in need of a visit to the bushes – yes, your rotten fish is still in my system – but by the sound of those sirens, the constabulary will be here very soon."

The sirens wailed ever closer.

"Very well." I reached into my memory, focusing on the words I'd copied into my grimoire, seeing them written on the page in my mind's eye. I recited the ancient words and as I did so, a wisping trail of ember-like energy rose from my mouth and wound its way to Neil. Vines loosened, releasing his jaw, and the flashes of burnt orange light sank onto his tongue.

"Tell me, Neil Montpellier, why you murdered the women on the moors."

He shook his head, his eyes bulging, but the words flowed easily from his mouth. "For my wife. She was devastated when she discovered that Heather Norton believed her father was the killer and that Leonard Dimmock was innocent. She turned into a monster and took out her rage on me. She'd always been difficult, but that flipped her over the edge, and she made my life hell again. It brought back the worst in her and I've spent so many years trying to keep it at a manageable level. I thought if I could make people believe that Leonard was killing again, our life could go back to normal. Heather knew too much, so she had to go first."

"See! I was right!" crowed Lucifer. "He did it for his wife."

"He did it for himself," Garrett corrected. "To stop his wife abusing him."

Neil flashed scared eyes towards his bound wife. "She's not easy to live with," he said.

"She has a history of violence, threats of violence, and stalking," Garrett explained. "Her dad used to clear up any mess—pulled a few strings to make any charges go away, but she has form."

Neil remained silent and closed his eyes.

"I had no idea. Poor man!" I said.

"It's no excuse for killing innocent people, Liv," said Garrett.

"You're right, it's not," I agreed. "But he's afraid of her."

"Still no excuse. He could have left her. There were plenty of opportunities over the years. People tried to help him."

"Still ..."

"People are complex, but he's got what he wants now."

"How?"

"She won't be able to abuse him where he's going."

As Garrett spoke, three police cars pulled into the yard, and I retracted the binding spell.

With Neil and Karyn Montpellier safely handcuffed and in the custody of the police, we watched the cars pull out of the yard. Garrett slipped an arm across my back and pulled me to his side before bending to kiss me.

Epilogue

Several weeks passed with Garrett and I spending what spare time we had together. We finally had afternoon tea with Uncle Tobias along with Finn and Jofrid who had moved into Blackwood Manor. With their lives in danger, and the threat of their child being kidnapped a very real prospect, I was tasked with creating a protective spell around the estate to help conceal their whereabouts, and we all waited with anticipation upon the arrival of their child whilst I secretly wondered if it would come out dark, hairy, and a full set of teeth with particularly long canines.

At home, I paid more than my usual attention to my aunts and began to take serious interest in learning what knowledge they had to offer.

"What do I do now?" I asked, stirring a large pot on the stove. Inside, liquid swirled—my own recipe for a calmative that had come to me as my fairy friend had buzzed around my head one morning at the shop.

"Recite the charm and follow the instructions I've written down on the paper, then remove it from the heat and let it cool," instructed Aunt Euphemia.

As I stirred the pot three times to the left and then three times to the right whilst reciting the charm that had come to me during a moment of clarity, a wave of intense energy passed through the room.

"Whatever was that?" asked Aunt Thomasin as she stepped out of the pantry. "Did you feel it?"

"I did, sister. There is something amiss."

"Indeed. I feel it in my bones."

"I felt it too," I said, shivering to shake off the chill that had passed over me. "It felt as though it came through the front of the house."

"Then there must be something outside."

"But the protective shield is up, is it not?"

"I renewed it last night."

"So it is not a hex."

"It could be, if whoever threw it got through our defences."

Aunt Thomasin shook her head. "I didn't feel like a hex."

"I took it as a warning—the arrival of a portent."

I removed the elixir from the heat and turned off the stove. "I'm going outside to check. If there's something out there, I want to know what it is. If someone is attacking us again, they'll find us ready this time."

"That's the spirit, dear," said Aunt Beatrice as she entered the room. "But who is attacking us?"

"We don't know if anyone is, but we all felt a distinct wave of energy."

"You too?" asked Aunt Beatrice. "I thought there was something, but presumed it was Livitha's efforts going belly-up—again."

"Thanks!"

"It came from outside, Beatrice."

"Oh!"

"Exactly."

"I'm going to check," I said, taking off my apron as I moved towards the kitchen door.

Outside the winter sun was bright in a clear sky and my breath billowed white in the cold as I made my way around the house. Checking across the driveway and into the trees I could feel and see nothing untoward but as I turned the corner to the front of the house the door opened, and I heard Aunt Thomasin exclaim in surprise.

I picked up my pace and ran to the door. A large box sat on the doorstep. "What is it?"

"A baby," stated Aunt Thomasin.

"You're kidding!" I said as I reached the steps.

Aunt Thomasin was joined by Euphemia and Beatrice and all three stared down into the box where a tiny baby swaddled in a white blanket, its head protected from the cold by a tiny knitted white hat, lay.

"There's a note." Aunt Thomasin made no effort to stoop and pick it up.

After several more seconds of staring at the baby, incredulous that it had been left on our doorstep with no sign of the mother, or father, I reached in to take the note.

"What does it say?"

"Give her a minute, she's only just picked it up!"

I unfolded the note. Buzzing vibrated in my wrist.

"So, what does it say?"

"It says ..." I faltered, my breathe taken from me. "It says, 'The Beast is yours to keep.'"

"What?"

"Whatever does that mean?"

I crouched beside the box and lifted the baby out, marvelling at its beauty but, as I held it in the crook of my arm, the dragon, bird, and boar on my bangle began to writhe and I remembered Aunt Loveday's warning that the creatures came alive when there was an existential threat to the coven.

***

THE END

***

Stay Informed

Stay up to date with JCs newest releases by signing up to her reader group. You'll be the first to know what's coming up and receive an email to your inbox on publication day.

Sign up at the website: www.jcblake.com[1]

Or join here: JC Blake's Newsletter[2]

***

Other Books by the Author

Meet Liv and her fascinating aunts in this addictive series

Menopause, Magick, & Mystery

Hormones, Hexes, & Exes[3]

Hot Flashes, Sorcery, & Soulmates[4]

Night Sweats, Necromancy, & Love Bites[5]

Menopause, Moon Magic, & Cursed Kisses[6]

Midlife Hexes & Gathering Storms[7]

---

1.   http://www.jcblake.com

2.   https://dl.bookfunnel.com/pgh4acj6f8

3. https://books2read.com/u/3yKEzv

4. https://books2read.com/u/baDnaa

5. https://books2read.com/u/31RGYl

6. https://books2read.com/u/meng79

7. https://books2read.com/u/mvWQ22

***

Meet Leofe, the Poison Garden Witch, as she discovers her magical powers and makes life after divorce an adventure.
<u>Deadheading the Hemlock</u>[8]

***

A young woman pushed to the edge of a breakdown in this supernatural murder mystery.
<u>When the Dead Weep</u>[9]

***

8. https://books2read.com/u/bOzxKE

9. https://books2read.com/u/mKpDyd

Printed in Great Britain
by Amazon

19852375R00140